TAKING OFF

THE PERSONAL HISTORY,
ADVENTURES, EXPERIENCES
& OBSERVATIONS
OF
PETER LEROY

BY ERIC KRAFT

(so far)

Little Follies

Herb 'n' Lorna

Reservations Recommended

Where Do You Stop?

What a Piece of Work I Am

At Home with the Glynns

Leaving Small's Hotel

Inflating a Dog

Passionate Spectator

TAKING OFF

ERIC KRAFT

St. Martin's Press  New York

www.stmartins.com

www.erickraft.com/peterleroy

Author's notes: The illustrations on the cover and pages 48 and 185 are adaptations of an illustration by Stewart Rouse that first appeared on the cover of the August 1931 issue of *Modern Mechanics and Inventions*. The boy at the controls of the aerocycle doesn't particularly resemble Peter Leroy — except, perhaps, for the smile. The passage from *Antique Scandals* on page 40 is a fabrication; as far as I know, no such book exists. The photograph on page 43 is from *Elements of Aeronautics,* by Francis Pope and Arthur S. Otis, copyright © 1941 by the World Book Company. The page from *Impractical Craftsman* on page 49 is an adaptation of a page from the August 1931 issue of *Modern Mechanics and Inventions.* The advertisement for Dædalus Welding on page 78 is based on an advertisement for Hohner Harmonicas that appeared in the September 1937 issue of *Modern Mechanix.* "Build a Power Saw from Scrap Parts" on page 102 is based on an article in the May 1936 issue of *Modern Mechanix & Inventions.* The frontispiece from *Elements of Aeronautics* reproduced on page 131 is, in fact, the frontispiece from *Elements of Aeronautics.* Peter's conversation with the neighborhood character known as Baudelaire on pages 189 and 190 is based on a passage in Baudelaire's *The Painter of Modern Life,* translated by Jonathan Mayne, and the photograph of the neighborhood character is in fact Nadar's 1863 portrait of Baudelaire. Except for those credited above, all illustrations have been cobbled together by the author from clip art and his own photographs.

ISBN 0-312-31884-7
EAN 978-0-312-31884-0

First Edition: July 2006

10 9 8 7 6 5 4 3 2 1

For Mad

I'd often dreamed of going West to see the country, always vaguely planning and never taking off.
    Jack Kerouac, *On the Road*

TAKING OFF

Preface
Lets and Hindrances, Views and Prospects

When a man sits down to write a history,—tho' it be but the history of Jack Hickathrift or Tom Thumb, he knows no more than his heels what lets and confounded hindrances he is to meet with in his way,—or what a dance he may be led, by one excursion or another, before all is over. . . . For, if he is a man of the least spirit, he will have fifty deviations from a straight line to make with this or that party as he goes along, which he can no ways avoid. He will have views and prospects to himself perpetually soliciting his eye, which he can no more help standing still to look at than he can fly. . . .
    Laurence Sterne, *Tristram Shandy*

IN THE SUMMER OF MY FIFTEENTH YEAR, I made a solo flight from Babbington, New York, on the South Shore of Long Island, to Corosso, New Mexico, in the foothills of the San Mateo Mountains, on the banks of the Rio Grande, in a single-seat airplane that I had built in the family garage. Because I was still a boy, barely a teenager, the feat was breathlessly recounted in the Babbington newspaper, the *Reporter,* and in the regional press as well. There were errors in those reports, and the errors have been repeated in anniversary recaps at intervals since then. The errors have now been so fully sanctioned by repetition that they have the ring of truth. From time to time my day is interrupted by phone calls from eager interviewers who want me to tell the story again. Without exception, they want me to retell the story as it has already been reported. I have tried, during some of those telephone interviews, to correct a few errors of fact and interpretation, but my efforts have been dismissed with the condescending politeness that we employ with those whom we regard as having had their wits enfeebled by time.

Because I have consistently failed to set the record straight by phone, I have for some time intended to prepare a full and accurate written account that would do the job without my having to pause in the telling to endure the protests of reporters who accuse me of being "modest" when I am only trying to be, at long last, honest. I have finally begun writing that account. The first third of it, which chronicles my preparations for the trip, occupies the pages that follow, and to my surprise, it *is* full and accurate, setting a standard of completeness and accuracy that I shall strive to maintain in the two parts of the tale that are still to come.

In the spirit of completeness and accuracy, I will confess to you here that the account that I have found myself writing is not quite the account that I had intended to provide. I'll be frank: I had not intended to set the record quite so straight as I have done. I had intended to allow some of the old errors to stand—the ones that conveyed an impression of me as more capable and my trip as more successful than either actually was—and I had intended to perpetuate the myth of myself as a daring flyboy, the "Birdboy of Babbington," the epitome of American ingenuity and pluck, teen division. My intentions altered after I revisited Babbington, the start and finish of that famous flight.

As you will see in Chapter 1, "Babbington Needs Me," I revisited the town because I received a note from a former schoolmate urging me to see what had become of the place during my absence.

Following that visit, upon my return to Manhattan, I sat down to write, full of good intentions, determined, focused, a man with a mission. Almost at once I began to meet with lets and confounded hindrances, difficulties and disappointments, and even a personal disaster—an injury to my beloved Albertine—that delayed my work, stretching it out over a far longer time than I had intended to give it. This unexpected extension of the time given to thinking about what I wanted to say led me to compose a more complete account than I had intended. For me, you see, the lets and hindrances abetted my love for a full account, because they gave me time, and, given time, I tend to wander, and when I wander the byways of memory, surprising views and prospects solicit my eye. I pause. I look. I enjoy the view. I explore the prospects. I add the view or prospect to my account. I can't help myself. I am by nature digressive, within limits.

My friend Mark Dorset, an unaffiliated academic who specializes in human motivation, has written at some length on digression, and some of what he has said applies to me:

> Digression is antithetical to, but dependent on, the intention to progress along the straight and narrow way. In order to digress, one must first be progressing. One cannot be sidetracked unless one is first on track. One cannot stray unless one is first on the right path. One cannot turn aside unless one is first moving straight ahead. Proust famously pointed out that we cannot remember what has not occurred; he might just as well have pointed out that we cannot digress from a route that we had not intended to take.
>
> If one's honest answer to the question "Where are you trying to go?" is "I don't know," then one cannot digress.
>
> To digress, then, you must begin by traveling a route that will get you where you intend to go. You must have a goal and a plan for achieving it in order to depart from it. You cannot digress from the right path unless you are already on it.
>
> The easiest path to digress from is the straight and narrow, the straight and strait, rather than the broad way that rambles on its own. The slightest deviation from the straight and narrow is a digression, but the broad way allows a lot of wandering within it, so that one may amble a meandering course and still be within its limits, not really digressing at all.
>
> The digressive thinker is by nature an explorer rather than a point-A-to-point-B traveler. What is the opposite of a digressive thinker? Someone like Phileas Fogg as Jules Verne portrayed him in *Around the World in Eighty Days*:
>
>> He gave the idea of being perfectly well-balanced, as exactly regulated as a Leroy chronometer. . . .
>> He was so exact that he was never in a hurry, was always ready, and was economical alike of his steps and his motions. He never took one step too many, and always went to his des-

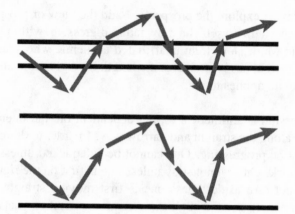

The slightest deviation from the straight and narrow is a digression [top], but the broad way allows a lot of wandering within it [bottom], so that one may amble a meandering course and still be within its limits, not really digressing at all.

tination by the shortest cut; he made no superfluous gestures, and was never seen to be moved or agitated. He was the most deliberate person in the world, yet always reached his destination at the exact moment.

He lived alone, and, so to speak, outside of every social relation; and as he knew that in this world account must be taken of friction, and that friction retards, he never rubbed against anybody.

That is certainly not me. I am no Phileas Fogg. I rub against everybody—and against every memory—and against everybody in every memory. The friction retards my progress but warms my heart.

Mark continues:

There is attached to digression a strong suggestion of weakness of character in the digresser. The digresser is digressive, inclined to stray from the right path, the point, the main subject, the intended direction, and the goal, and this tendency to stray is considered by many to be a fault, which characterization makes digression nearly equal to transgression. Progression, on the other hand, is generally regarded as a virtue. The progresser, if you will allow me the term, is progressive (not in the political sense, usually, but in the forward-marching sense), never straying from the path or plan, always moving toward an established goal step by step. To go off course by choice, or to be lured from the right path by a seductive roadside attraction, is regarded as a fault, but to be forced off course is not. The sailor blown off course by mighty Aeolus is guiltless, a victim, but the sailor drawn off course by the Sirens' song is a fool who ought to have stopped his ears with wax and stayed the course.

I was, as I hope you will agree after reading the pages that follow, blown off course by the accident of Albertine's injury as much as I was lured off course by the siren call of unsolicited recollection. The first was no fault of mine, an accident. The second I count a virtue, since it served the cause of completeness and accuracy. As a result, however, the short book that I had intended to write about my exploit has become three books, the Flying trilogy: *Taking Off* (in which I make my plans and depart), *On the Wing* (in which I meander from Babbington to New Mexico), and *Flying Home* (in which I return to Babbington, somewhat older and, perhaps, somewhat the wiser).

Peter Leroy
New York City
January 25, 2006

Chapter 1
Babbington Needs Me

I WAS BORN AND RAISED IN BABBINGTON, a small town situated on the South Shore of Long Island, lying between the eastern border of Nassau County and the western border of Suffolk County. (Actually, I was born in the hospital in neighboring South Hargrove, since there was no hospital in Babbington, but that made mine a birth so close to being born in Babbington as not to matter.) My roots in the town reach a couple of generations down into its sandy soil, deep roots for an American family. Babbington formed me: I was a Babbington boy. I enjoyed my childhood there, but, like many other small-town boys, I began to want to leave the place in my adolescence. During junior year in high school, a friend of mine, Matthew Barber, had the good fortune to win a scholarship to a summer institute sponsored by the National Preparedness Foundation. It was to be held at the New Mexico College of Agriculture, Technology, and Pharmacy, in Corosso. Matthew's winning the scholarship inspired in me a fierce envy and an even fiercer determination to get to Corosso myself. By giving me a destination, Matthew's acceptance at the summer institute justified my building an airplane, an undertaking that my father might otherwise not have been willing to allow—certainly not in the family garage—and by taking me such a distance from home, my trip to Corosso gave me the taste of a wider world that I had come to crave.

While sampling that wider world, I was surprised to find how much I missed Babbington and how much I measured the rest of the world by the standards and peculiarities of my home town. Later in life, in college, and later still, during my brief experience of conventional work, the larger world made a further impression on me, but I persisted in interpreting it

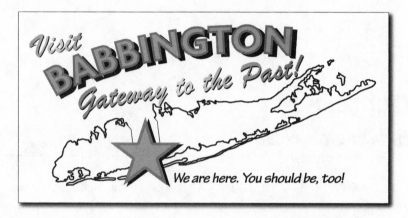

Then, not long ago, I received a postcard . . .

by translating it into the familiar terms of the small world of Babbington and my childhood experiences there. Late in my twenties, I returned to Babbington, with the intention of staying. My wife, Albertine, and I worked at one job and another to accumulate enough for a down payment on Small's Hotel, and when a surprise bequest from the estate of an old bayman, "Cap'n" Andrew Leech, gave us the last bit that we lacked, we put our money down and bought it. For the next couple of decades we tried to make a success of Small's, but in the end the sum of our success was that we were able to sell it, pay our debts, and escape with a small amount of equity. We moved to Manhattan, where we live now, with the intention that we would return to Babbington often. Albertine has relatives living in the neighboring towns, and for me the place has the draw of a spiritual home, the place where the heart lies. I fully expected that in Manhattan I would be homesick for Babbington, as I had been so often during my trip to New Mexico, but I was not. I kept intending to return, but my intention was inspired more by feelings of obligation than by desire. I felt that I ought to visit certain old friends and acquaintances, ought to see how the hotel was faring under the management of its new owners, ought to go clamming, just to keep my hand in, and yet, however much I felt that I *ought* to go, I never quite managed to get around to going.

Years passed. The Long Island Rail Road continued to run trains to Babbington at convenient hours daily, but I never took one, never attempted to go home again. In a very short time, Manhattan became my home, my playground, my seat of operations. I had been a Babbington boy, but I had become a man of Manhattan, a part of the great urban crowd.

Then, not long ago, I received a postcard from a woman who had lived in Babbington throughout her childhood and youth, as I had, a coeval named Cynthia, who had been called Cyn or Sin or even Sinful when she and I were classmates in elementary school and high school. During the critical formative years of our lives, we had been suckled on the culture of Babbington, in circumstances that were nearly identical. However, Cyn had remained in Babbington after high school, had married a Babbington boy, was still living in Babbington, and had no intention of leaving.

Her message was brief but unsettling.

Peter,

I wish you would return to Babbington and see what they are doing to our town. It's enough to make your flesh crawl. If you can possibly get here on Friday the 29th, at around five, I'll meet you at the bar at Legends restaurant in the "Historic Downtown Plaza." Please come. Babbington needs you.

Cynthia

Her words dealt me a stab of guilt, for they inspired within me the feeling that I had betrayed the town by leaving it. I would have to return. I would have to see what "they" were doing to the place. I would have to see what I could do to make things right.

Chapter 2
In the Historic Downtown Plaza

Already the teaching of Tlön's harmonious history (filled with
moving episodes) has obliterated the history that governed my own
childhood; already a fictitious past has supplanted in men's memories that other past, of which we now know nothing certain—not
even that it is false.

Jorge Luis Borges, postscript to "Tlön, Uqbar, Orbis Tertius"

THUS IT WAS that, late in the afternoon of the Friday following my receipt of Cyn's note, Albertine and I found ourselves seated side by side
aboard a Long Island Rail Road train bound for Babbington, where, for
me, it had all begun. Albertine was with me because she and I are together whenever it is possible for us to be together. We discovered long
ago that the point of our lives is to be together, so we try to avoid all individual experience, within the limits of practicality and gracious living.
This practice has brought us as close as any two people can be, I think. It
also allows her to keep an eye on me.

"I have no idea what the 'Historic Downtown Plaza' might be," said
Albertine, who knows the town as well as I do.

"I picked up this brochure in the station," I said, handing the brochure
to Albertine. "It promotes excursions to Babbington. The writer attempts
to explain the Historic Downtown Plaza, but the explanation doesn't suc-
ceed in clarifying it."

The brochure was titled "Babbington: Gateway to the Past." It bore the logo of the Babbington Redefinition Authority, and it described my home town in the following manner:

> The delightful town of Babbington is the Central South Shore's nostalgia center—or, if not precisely its center, not far off the mark. Babbington offers fine accommodations, restaurants, its own historic charm, and many fascinating attractions and diversions.
>
> The Historic Downtown Plaza, a pedestrian mall lined with buildings dating from the 1950s and even earlier, serves as one of the major "destinations" for Babbingtonians and "out-of-towners" alike.
>
> Downtown employees and shoppers frequent the Plaza to have lunch or stroll through the variety of shops, to slip out of the drudgery of everyday life in the early twenty-first century and back into the blissful middle of the twentieth. The beautifully landscaped Plaza provides a setting for town festivals such as the Clam Fest, traditionally held on the first weekend of May. Highlight of the weeklong extravaganza is the crowning of Miss Clam Fest. Despite the controversy that has plagued the Fest for the last several years, it still draws an enthusiastic crowd. The clam-fritter-eating contest is always exciting and tense. Deaths have occurred.
>
> The Babbington Redefinition Authority is hard at work to make Babbington everything it might once have been. In Babbington you will find the perfect starting point for your passport to the past, the perfect place to start or end your day.

"'The perfect starting point for your passport to the past'?" said Albertine. "What on earth does that mean?"

"Oh, it's just somebody's attempt to squirt a little of the flavor of foreign travel onto a visit to Babbington," I said.

"That somebody has confused *passport* and *passage,* I think."

"Probably a fellow graduate of Babbington High," I muttered, rescuing the poor pamphlet from her before she picked any other little nits of illiteracy from it.

"Sorry," she said. "I forgot how touchy you are about—"

"Here we are," I said. "Let's find out why my town needs me."

ALBERTINE AND I found the Historic Downtown Plaza easily enough. It was a T-shaped stretch of Upper Bolotomy Road and Main Street at the center of town. Two blocks of Upper Bolotomy and four blocks of Main (two to the east of the intersection and two to the west) had been closed to vehicular traffic, though there were cars parked at the curb. I admired some of these as I walked along, because they were handsome examples of the cars that had been the objects of my adolescent car-lust when I was in high school.

"Wow," I said in exactly the tone of awestruck reverence I would have used when I was too young to drive.

"Watch where you're going," Al cautioned me, taking hold of my arm and steering me away from a collision with a vintage lamppost.

"Did you see that car we just passed?" I asked. "A 1956 Golden Hawk. Two-hundred-seventy-five horsepower and Ultramatic Drive."

"But not much of a back seat," she said with a wink and a leer. With a sigh for days gone by, we went in search of the restaurant called Legends.

It would have been hard to miss. It announced itself with a large neon sign that bore its name and the slogan "Portal to the Plaza." A smaller sign beside the door offered "Our Incomparable Happy Hour" Monday through Friday, 4:30 P.M. to 6:30 P.M., featuring free hors d'oeuvres and "special drink prices."

The restaurant was just at the northern limit of the plaza in a space that had been filled by a large grocery store when Al and I were kids. The interior had been turned into a miniature shopping mall, with skylights overhead, giving it some of the feeling of a suburban shopping mall, but on a compact scale. Legends occupied the center, and the surrounding area was filled with shops, kiosks, and pushcarts stocked with souvenirs, gewgaws, and "antiques" from approximately the time when Albertine and I were spending Saturday nights in the back seat of her parents' Lark sedan, parked among the concealing rushes at the edge of Bolotomy Bay.

A small group had gathered at the circular bar for the incomparable happy hour. They all seemed to be regulars. They sat and drank. Now and then they spoke to one another. One of their number was addressed by the others as "Judge." The free hors d'oeuvres on this evening were potato chips and a bowl of clam dip.

"Amazing," I said after sampling the dip. "This could have been made from my mother's recipe."

A younger woman came in, apparently stopping by after work, climbed onto a barstool, crossed her eye-catching legs, and ordered a Tom Collins.

"A Tom Collins," I whispered to Al. "When was the last time you heard anybody order a Tom Collins?"

"Nineteen sixty-one," said Albertine, "in the summer, the night we crashed that party in—"

"Shhh," I said with a finger to my lips, and we settled into the poses we assume when indulging in silent eavesdropping.

The happy-hour drinkers were talking of an approaching storm, Hurricane Felicity. Thousands had been evacuated from the New Jersey Shore, one of them noted. Tens of thousands more were without power in that area, according to another. Weekend plans were off, announced the woman with the Tom Collins.

"Hurricane Felicity," I whispered to Al. "There was a Hurricane Felicity when we were in high school, wasn't there?"

"There was," she said.

"Al," I said, "this place is—"

Chapter 3
The Birdboy of Babbington

JUST THEN, CYNTHIA ARRIVED. She seemed to be wearing a disguise, having gotten herself up as a woman of a certain age. "Hey, there," she said, in the breathy come-hither-big-boy voice that had inspired her teenage nicknames, "if it isn't the Birdbrain of Babbington in the flesh."

"That's Birdboy, Sinful."

"Birdboy to your face, but it was always Birdbrain behind your back."

"It was?" I asked. "Are you serious? Or are you just making that up? I never knew that anyone—"

"My goodness!" she exclaimed. "Albertine! Look at you, girl. You're gorgeous! *Still* gorgeous, I should say. What did you do, make a pact with the devil?"

"How sweet of you—"

"Come here," said Cynthia, taking our drinks and leading us away from the bar to the table farthest from it. When she had us arranged as she wanted us, she leaned toward the center of the table, dropped her voice to a hoarse whisper, and said, "Let's get to the point." She glanced from side to side to see if anyone was listening. "They're turning this town into a theme park," she said. "It's enough to gag a maggot."

"They?" I asked.

"The BRA."

"The Babbington Redefinition Authority," I said.

"You've done your homework. Good. You see those people at the bar? They're actors. Playing the part of residents. Paid by the BRA."

"Are you saying that they're actors?" I asked.

"Birdbrain—"

"I mean, are they professionals?"

"I was speaking in the broadest sense," she said, rolling her eyes.

"Of course," I said. "Forgive me. From time to time, my keen and hard-won adult acumen is replaced by the naïveté of a boy who lives somewhere within me, a child, or the remnants of a child, who yearns for things to be simpler than they are, and I forget that people rarely mean quite what they say."

She gave me a very odd look. Then she went on. "They are actual residents of the town—when they're offstage, so to speak—but right now they're actors, *playing* residents of the town," she said.

"I see," I said. "Of course. You were speaking in the broadest sense, figuratively, not literally." I paused. Then I said, "I don't have any idea what you're talking about."

"Did you walk through the 'Historic Downtown Plaza'?"

"A bit."

"What did you think?"

"It looks—the way I remember it—pretty much the way it was when we were kids here."

"Peter," she said, shaking her head at my denseness, "it's *exactly* the way it was when we were kids here, when we were in high school."

"Exactly?"

"As close as they could make it."

"Well, they seem to have done a good job—"

"They chose one day, the most fully documented day in the history of mid-twentieth-century Babbington, the one with the most available snapshots, news clippings, and anecdotes. In the Historic Downtown Plaza, they relive that day every day. Over and over. Ad nauseam."

"What day is that?"

"It's the day you flew back into town in that little airplane you built."

"It is?" Unbidden, a feeling of pride began to spread through me, and I think I may have blushed.

"That's what I said."

"So it's a form of historical drama that they're staging," I said, offhandedly, as if nothing I had ever done were involved in any way. "It seems harmless enough to me."

"You don't understand," she said, and she was almost pleading now. "It's spreading. It's spreading beyond the Historic Downtown Plaza, infecting the entire town, and all the residents in it. The BRA's efforts to make the town a more marketable version of itself have not been lost on residents outside the district of the re-enactment. They see the way the town is going, and they're eager to get in on the act. Babbington is not going to remain just-plain-Babbington. It's already well on the way to becoming Babbington™, Gateway to the Past®."

"What happened to 'Clam Capital of America'?" asked Albertine.

"It was officially declared 'unattractive.' I wish you could have been at the town meeting. I was eloquent. I invoked the Bolotomy tribe, shell mounds, wampum—"

"To no avail, I take it," I said.

She shook her head sadly, and turned a thumb down.

"They could have replaced it with 'Cradle of Teenage Solo Flight,'" I suggested.

Cynthia didn't laugh. With her eyes, she appealed to Albertine for support, and Al frowned at me.

Cyn rubbed her brow as if her head ached and said, "People all over town are coming to feel that in such a place as Babbington—that is, such a place as Babbington is becoming—it is not enough to be Jack Sprat, the local butcher; one must be Jack Sprat, Garrulous Butcher of Bygone Babbington, Gateway to the Past."

"I see," I said, wondering how she would describe herself in the list of town characters, what epithet she would attach to herself. "You said 'paid by the BRA,'" I reminded her.

"That, too, I meant in the broadest sense."

"Of course."

"The BRA is seeing to it that the only real business left in this town will be the business of being itself, though not really itself but an image of itself as it never was. To their credit, they have chosen a Babbington that's more like the earthy images of Brueghel the Elder than the kitsch of Norman Rockwell or Thomas Kinkade, but still they are turning the town into a simulation, and because that simulation is to be the engine of the town's economic recovery, everyone who agrees to participate in it is, in the broadest sense, on the payroll of the BRA."

"I see," I said again, thoughtfully, "and you say that all this is centered on my solo flight, my triumphant return, the parade—"

"Don't go feeling proud of yourself," she said. "You ought to be ashamed."

"You're right," I said. "I am." Still, in my silent thoughts I couldn't help wondering if it might not be possible to return to Babbington, become an actor in the BRA pageant, and play once again the part of Peter Leroy, Daring Flyboy. No. Of course not. Whoever played the Daring Flyboy would have to be considerably younger. A boy.

"Look," Cyn said suddenly, gathering her things, "I've got to go. There's a meeting of the Friends of the Bay that I've got to attend. But do me a favor. Take a walk around and look at the walls."

"The walls?"

"Haven't you noticed the walls here?"

"Here in the restaurant?"

"No, all over town. Of course I mean here in the restaurant. What's happened to your mind, Birdbrain?"

"He's often distracted," said Albertine. She may have been speaking in my defense.

"He's always been like that," said Cyn.

"And always will be," Albertine predicted.

"Drag him around the place to look at the walls, okay?"

"Okay."

"Promise?"

"Promise," said Albertine, woman to woman.

Cyn left in a rush. Before Albertine and I left Legends, we did as Al had promised we would do. We took a walk around the place and looked at the walls. They were covered, and that is nearly the truth, with caricatures of people who had been designated by the management of Legends as legendary figures in Babbington's past. I recognized many of them, and among them I recognized myself. Actually, Albertine recognized me first.

"Oh, no!" she squealed. "It's the Birdboy of Babbington."

There I was, celebrated and exaggerated, and there I stood, exhilarated and exasperated.

Albertine linked her arm with mine and hugged herself to me.

"Oh, that takes me back," she said warmly.

"Yes," I said, with considerably less enthusiasm. "It takes me back, too."

Chapter 4
Straight

MY SOLO FLIGHT. I have quite a mental scrapbook devoted to that flight. To be truthful, *flight* isn't quite the right word; *flights* would be more accurate, because it was not one continuous flight, though in the minds of most of those who remember it, or think that they remember it, it has come to be a continuous flight. I even think of it that way myself sometimes, as a nonstop flight from Babbington out to Corosso and another nonstop flight back. When I was interviewed upon my return, I tried to be honest about what I had accomplished and what I had not, but the interviewers had their own ideas about what the story ought to be, and nothing that I told them was going to change those ideas, so I began to go along with what they wanted. The account published in the *Reporter* was typical, an account that made the flight seem more than it actually was.

Babbington Boy Completes Solo Flight
Flies Cross-Country on His Own
Home-Built Plane Functions Flawlessly

Babbington — Peter Leroy will sleep in his own bed in Babbington Heights tonight, for the first time in more than two months, but you can bet that he'll have dreams of flying, as he has for as long as he can remember. We all have those dreams, said by some to be the remnants of our species' memory of swinging through the trees when we were apes, but most of us remain earthbound. Our flying is confined to our dreams. Not so for young Peter Leroy. This is a lad who makes his dreams come true.

"I found some plans for a plane in a magazine," he says, with disarming simplicity, "and I thought it would be fun to build it and fly it across the country."

The modesty of Babbington's aeronautical pioneer is charming. (Local politicians, please take note.) When asked by C. Nelson Dillwell, publisher of the *Reporter,* how he got to Corosso, New Mexico, some 1,800 miles from home, he responds, "Well, I flew," with a shrug, as if the feat were really nothing much more than a bike ride to the corner store to pick up a quart of milk for his mother. And how did you get back? "Flew," he says, with another shrug. When it is proposed to him that flying nearly 4,000 miles in a plane that he built in the garage of the modest Leroy family home is a significant feat, he grins the grin that has already won the hearts of all the secretaries at the *Reporter*'s spacious new downtown offices and says, "Well, I didn't fly all the way." What? You didn't fly all the way? "No," he says, shaking his head, apparently all seriousness. "I did some taxiing, before takeoffs, and then after landing, when I rolled along the ground for a way before coming to a stop." Ah, yes, let's set the record straight. Young Leroy did not fly

all the way to New Mexico and back. He did some taxiing and rolled along the runways a bit on landing. Noted.

YES, let's set the record straight. During my return trip, from Corosso to Babbington, I thought a lot about what I was going to say when I got home, and about the impression that my story would make, and I decided, quite deliberately, that I would be honest but not accurate. I would be honest overall but vague about the details. I intended to say that I had flown part of the way but not all the way. I don't recall when, in rehearsing my remarks, I began to refer to the earthbound portions of the trip as taxiing, but it was well before I came within sight of Babbington.

When I reached Babbington, I rolled into town along Main Street, coming from the west. There are people in Babbington to this day who will tell you that they saw me *fly* in from the west, make a lazy circle in the sky over the area now occupied by the Historic Downtown Plaza, and touch down near the park before rolling to a stop at the intersection of Bolotomy and Main, where the reviewing stand had been set up. Some of them honestly believe that they saw that landing, just as some people honestly believe that they have seen the ghost of a beloved aunt climbing the back staircase at midnight and others think that they have seen the silver spaceships of interstellar travelers flash in eerie swift silence across the night sky.

I was paraded up and down Main Street in the back seat of a convertible, with the mayor at the wheel and Miss Clam Fest at my side. People screamed my name as I passed. They threw streamers and confetti. I was given the key to the city. The high school band played "For He's a Jolly Good Fellow" again and again. Feeling like a jolly good fellow indeed, I went where I was led, into the building where the *Reporter* had its office, and found myself the subject of a press conference. All of the Babbington media were represented: the *Reporter,* of course; and the radio station, WCLM; as well as the Babbington high school paper, the *Esculent Mollusk.* All eyes were on me. My audience hung on my every word. I was the boy of the hour. I was completely intoxicated, drunk on fame, besotted with adulation.

The first question directed to me wasn't really a question at all. The publisher of the *Reporter,* who assumed control of the proceedings, said, as a preliminary to taking questions from the floor, "Peter, it is an honor for the *Reporter* to have you here today, and we all want to hear how you got from Babbington to New Mexico."

He paused, and I took his pause as my cue. Feeling even more full of myself than I ordinarily did, I said, "Well, I flew—"

I meant to add "part of the way." I really did.

However, when I said, "Well, I flew—" the response was immediate and overwhelming. People laughed. Then they applauded. Miss Clam Fest blew me a kiss from her seat in the front row. I added nothing to what I had said. I just shrugged. They loved it. They loved me. Miss Clam Fest in particular seemed to love me, even though she must have been a mature woman of twenty-two. I wasn't going to let the truth come between us. I told a version of the truth, as I had intended to, but it became a version that allowed people to believe what they so clearly wanted to believe, and what they wanted to believe was far from the version of the truth that I had planned to tell them.

I flew part of the way. That's true. As I carefully said later in the press conference, I also taxied part of the way, before taking off and upon landing. I would say now, years beyond the influence of Miss Clam Fest's strapless gown, based on the sober calculations of an essentially honest man, that I flew a total of about 180 to 200 feet on the way out to New Mexico. My longest sustained period of flight might have covered six feet. For the rest of the outbound trip, I was on the ground, "taxiing." On the way back, I flew nearly 1,800 miles, but I was a passenger in a Lockheed Constellation, and *Spirit of Babbington* was in the luggage compartment, disassembled, in crates. There. The record is straight.

Chapter 5
Oh, the Squalor

THE TRAIN ROLLED ON, carrying Albertine and me from Babbington to Manhattan, away from my past and toward our future. I noticed with a mixture of surprise and sadness how squalid the buildings beside the tracks were. All the businesses that the commercial buildings housed seemed to be involved in some sort of salvage, and the dwellings looked as if the passage of the trains so near had weakened them, made them list and tilt. Human life and all of its impedimenta began to seem senseless, fragile and impermanent, poorly made, like my life, like the story of my life, my rickety story.

"You're being quiet," said Albertine. "Is something bothering you?"

"Oh, no," I said. "Nothing."

"What is it?" she asked.

"You always know, don't you?"

"Always."

"I've been watching the scenery roll by, thinking about the squalor of it all, the way people mar the landscape, littering it with their junk, and I've been drawing the inevitable analogy between this landscape that we're passing through and the history of Babbington, the way I passed through that history, and the way I've littered it with my junk—"

"What junk would that be, exactly?"

"You know what I mean."

"Come on, Birdboy, speak your mind."

"The story of my solo flight to Corosso—"

"Are you calling that junk?"

"It's like one of those shacks along the tracks: rickety, jerry-built, cobbled together out of bits and pieces, not at all sturdy enough to—"

I didn't want to say it.

"Stand up under close scrutiny?" she suggested.

"Right," I said with a sigh.

"I see," she said. "And with the controversy that's developing over the redefinition of the town, some bright young reporter is going to start investigating the central and essential legend—"

"—the Legend of the Birdboy of Babbington—"

"—and discover that the legendary birdboy has wings of clay."

"That's it."

"Then you'd better get to work."

"On a cover-up?"

"A full and frank disclosure, I think."

Chapter 6
Dreams of Flying

___

I HAD DREAMS in which I flew, of course. I still do. The manner of my flying in those dreams, and the style of my flying, has not changed with the passage of time. In my dreams, as a man, I fly as I flew as a boy. Essentially, I drift. Most often I jump from a height—a cliff, a balcony, a bridge—and I drift slowly toward the ground. I am able to will myself forward, but I remain upright, or nearly upright, in the position I would expect to land in, prepared to plant my feet on the ground. I seem always about to land, to come to earth, though I may keep drifting forward, or gliding forward, for a long time, covering quite a bit of distance. I never seem to begin a flight with the intention of going forward, or going in any horizontal direction at all. I seem to intend only to let myself drop slowly, safely, gifted as I am with the power of flight, from a high place to a lower place. Traveling, getting somewhere in some direction, seems to come along as an afterthought, almost as if, once dropping slowly in my controlled fashion, I let myself be carried by a breeze, or by an inclination. Part of the pleasure of these dreams seems to come from this accidental aspect of flight, the notion that it seems to free me not only from the weight imposed by gravity but from the purposefulness imposed by a destination. I do not fly to get anywhere, but only to be a flier, or—simpler still—I fly because I am a flier.

I also had *daydreams* of flying, waking dreams, wishes and fantasies, but they were quite different from my sleeping dreams of flying. My daydreams were about getting somewhere, or about getting away from where I was and flying to somewhere else. They were about escape and exploration, and they were deliberate. I launched my daydreams as I might have launched a flying machine. I got into the dream and took off. Often I launched one of these daydreams on a Sunday, when I was in the back seat of the family car, and my family was out for a Sunday drive.

There were parkways on Long Island, highways built to resemble country roads, with bridges faced with rustic-cut stone, wooden railings and wooden dividers between the opposite lanes, light poles of wood, and landscaping that was designed to look as if the hand of man had not been involved in it. Parkways were ideal for a Sunday drive, the next best thing to a country road. These parkways still exist, but the density of the traffic has made them less attractive for a Sunday drive. The density of traffic has made the whole concept of the Sunday drive less attractive.

On either side of the parkway's roadway, running alongside it, there was a pathway. I think that I am right in saying that I never saw anyone walking along one of those pathways, and it occurs to me now that the paths may have been provided more as an element of landscaping than as a way that was intended for actual use by hikers or bicyclists. They were, perhaps, intended to heighten or strengthen the impression of driving along a country road by evoking the notion of a footpath that one might walk or hike with rucksack and alpenstock, or to provide the expectation that one might while driving see someone else doing the hiking, a generous someone who thus completed the country-road impression while allowing the driver and passengers to remain comfortably seated in the family car.

For the boy sitting in the back seat of *my* family's car, the pathway was more interesting than the roadway. It wandered a bit, for one thing. The road may have been made to resemble a country road, but its route had been laid out to eliminate as far as possible anything that stood in the driver's way, including the hills and turns that make a country road a pleasant meander. The land beside the roadway had not been flattened as the roadway had. In fact, I think that if I were to take the trouble to do the research, I would find that it had been deliberately contoured to give the illusion of land in a natural state, uneven, untamed, and that when the little pathway had been built the landscapers had made it meander, within limits, like a miniature of the country road that the parkway was intended to suggest. The path had its ups and downs, its meanders and rambles and digressions. It had stretches that seemed a bit off course. Now and then it would disappear from view behind a clump of trees, becoming all the more attractive for having disappeared.

As we rolled along the parkway, I followed the pathway with my eyes, and in my daydreams I imagined moving along the pathway in a kind of hovercraft. It rose no more than a couple of feet above the surface, but it flew, though I have no idea how. As it flew, it was utterly silent, since it was powered by wishful thinking, by my powerfully propulsive wish to be out of the back seat of the family car.

Chapter 7
On Intention and Travel

ALBERTINE AND I ROLLED ON, in the stutter step of a Long Island Rail Road commuter train, making all the stops. I sat beside the window, looking out, daydreaming. There was no rambling path beside us, but my daydreams no longer need the stimulus of a rambling path. These days, I ramble most of the time, though I rarely go anywhere.

"I wish we could go somewhere now," I said to Al suddenly. "Right now, this minute."

"Where do you want to go?" she asked lazily. She was curled on her side with her head on my shoulder, trying to doze.

"Nowhere," I said truthfully, "or anywhere. I am convinced that the best travel is travel undertaken without a destination, just wandering. I am not the first to say that the slower the traveler goes, the more he sees. If I could, I would set out now and walk, hither and yon, following a course like that of the river Mæander."

"Why don't we?"

"Because we're tethered here."

"Can't we loose the surly bonds?"

"Not until we've paid our debts and put enough aside to finance a ramble and the time that it would take."

"But we'll have that goal?"

"Yes. The goal of traveling without a goal."

"It's our intention. Shall we put this in writing and ink the pact?"

"Let's just say it out loud and shake on it. Or make love on it."

"It is our intention to work very, very hard to pay off our debts and put some money aside and then to walk out our door on the way to nowhere."

"Without a map, without a destination."

"But every night we'll stop somewhere to have a hot shower, a fabulous meal, and a dreamy sleep in a comfy bed."

"If possible."

"I'm going to insist on that."

"But that means that we would have a destination—actually, a series of destinations—a destination for every night."

"Even the river Mæander winds somewhere safe to sea."

Chapter 8
One in a Line of Impractical Craftsmen

THE LOW-FLYING VEHICLE of my daydreams, strong, swift, and silent, was derived from an article in *Impractical Craftsman* magazine. I was a faithful reader of this magazine. So was my father. Both of my grandfathers were subscribers, and they had made many projects from plans published in its pages or ordered from its Projects Department. I had made a couple of things from *Impractical Craftsman* plans myself. They gave me satisfaction, not only the satisfaction of having completed a job, made a thing, but also the satisfaction of taking my place in the family line of impractical craftsmen. Dædalus was the household god of *Impractical Craftsman.* The masthead of each issue included a small drawing of him (with his disobedient son beside him), and the best of the projects in the magazine were truly daedal: ingenious, cleverly intricate, and diversified.

My father had also made things from plans in *IC,* as its devotees called it, but he tended to prefer the plans in other, less visionary, magazines for backyard builders, and he would usually build useful, boring things like bedside tables and chests of drawers rather than the marginally useful but intriguingly complicated mechanical, electromechanical, and electronic gadgets that my grandfathers and I favored.

I am wronging my father somewhat by suggesting that some shortcoming made him the sort of person who lacked the daring to venture beyond making simple pine tables and chests. Certainly he fell short of my grandfathers, and even of me, in his willingness to undertake a project that promised long periods of baffling, exacting work and little chance of success, but he wasn't entirely immune to the desire to stretch himself out into the realm of the unbuildable. I recall that he became excited about an *IC* project that, if it had been completed successfully, would have resulted in an early form of wireless television remote control. He never succeeded in getting the device to work, and it "plagued" him, as my mother moaned when he sank into a blue funk over his failure. As I recall the gadget, it wasn't going to do anything more than turn the television set on and off and raise or lower the volume. Before my father began this project, I had already built, from a kit advertised in the back pages of *IC,* an "electric eye" that would have done the job of turning the set on and off and could have been triggered by a flashlight from my father's chair, which would have qualified it as a wireless remote control, so it seemed to me that I could have solved half of his problem without really trying, and I felt a brief superiority until I began to try to figure out how the electric eye could be modified to control the volume and saw how much more difficult that was. My father dismantled the device that he had built and reassembled it several times, checking off the steps in the article systematically each time, but never could make it work. He banished it to a spot on the bottom shelf of his huge, cluttered workbench in the basement, but the anticipation of reaching a goal, a destination, had infected him with determination, and now he could not stop thinking about the idea of remote control for the television set. He would sit in his favorite chair, watching television, dreaming of a way to control it from where he sat, chewing the bitter cud of failure.

My father must have been one of the country's greatest television enthusiasts in those early days. His chair sagged nearly to the floor from the thousands of hours he had spent in it, pursuing his hobby. If the industry had known about his devotion to the medium, its captains would probably have rewarded him somehow. They might have given him a dinner. They might have given him a remote control, if they had one that worked.

One evening, while he sat there watching and brooding, the thought dawned on my father that he could achieve remote control if he simply removed the essential controls from the cabinet that held the television set, extended the wires that connected them to the rest of the circuitry, and placed them beside his favorite chair, where he could twiddle the dials at a distance from the set itself, remotely. Making the modifications was a

tedious task, but not a difficult one, and he accomplished it in a few evenings. He drilled a hole in the floor under the place where the set was
positioned and ran the wires through that hole. In the basement, he ran
them along the rafters to another hole under the position of his chair and
up through that hole to the living room, where he connected them to the
controls. To house the controls, he built a handsome pine box that he kept
at his side on the table between his chair and my mother's. He was a con-
tented man.

WHAT MY FATHER DID NOT REALIZE, and I did not realize, either,
was that some of the projects in *IC* were impossible to build. Though the
magazine emphasized projects that one could, presumably, actually build,
it also featured in every issue visionary articles about things that were not
buildable yet but might be buildable someday. There was a tension between the here-and-now projects, which had a crudeness about them that
made them achievable by the craftsman or hobbyist working in the basement or garage or back yard, and the sleek, seamless devices that were
forever just on the horizon, someday to be ours in our bright future of
swift transportation, gleaming gadgetry, and easy communication. The
visionary articles carried with them an inherent frustration. Always there
was at some point, toward the end, after the reader had become convinced
that the holographic teleportation device described in the article would
probably require no more than an afternoon's work, the almost casual
mention of technical lets and hindrances to its realization, mere details
that would "doubtless soon be solved" but stood in the way of attaining
the vision now. "In other words, Faithful Reader," the article quietly cautioned between its lines, "don't bother trying to build one of these holographic teleportation devices in your garage, because it won't work.
You'll run up against a wall of ignorance. We couldn't even do it here at
IC, in our world-famous Projects Development and Testing Laboratory."
In another magazine, articles of this you-couldn't-build-it-in-a-million-
years-sucker sort would not have included cutaway drawings, wiring diagrams, and accounts of the assembly of the device that could not be built,
but in *IC* they did. I now think that the zest for building, for making man-
ifest what the imagination had conjured in the mind, was so strong at *IC*
that the illustrators, writers, and editors who worked there found that they

could not prevent themselves from drawing pictures of the device and writing about its construction as if it had been built. They had, I suspect now, in an example of mass delusion, already convinced themselves that the thing *had* been built, that they had built it. This device that they had imagined *ought* to work, surely *would* work someday, and if that was so, as they believed it surely was, then one ought to be able to build it this way: Step 1 . . .

I suppose that most readers of *Impractical Craftsman* were adept at distinguishing between the two types of article. My father was not. Neither was I.

My friend Rodney Lodkochnikov, known as Raskolnikov or Raskol, was, in marked contrast, very good at distinguishing between the practicable, the doable, and the visionary, the as-yet undoable. When I showed him the article about the personal hovercraft and confessed to him that it was the flying machine of my daydreams, he took the magazine, glanced at the article and the accompanying drawings, and said, "This is great, but it's not the sort of thing you could build."

"I wasn't thinking of—" I began to protest.

"Yes, you were," he said, accurately.

Chapter 9
The Example of Dædalus and Icarus

THE THINKING at *Impractical Craftsman* was exactly the sort of thinking that got Dædalus and Icarus off the ground and into trouble.

In the words of Charles Mills Gayley, Dædalus was "a famous artificer." Gayley's *Classic Myths,* first published in 1893, was, along with *Ancient Myths for Modern Youth,* required reading in Mrs. Fendreffer's class, a class that was a rite of passage for all freshmen at Babbington High during my years there. Both texts sit on the bookshelf above my desk today.

The story of Dædalus's life is full of curiosities. This is how that story appeared in *Ancient Myths for Modern Youth*:

> We may as well acknowledge from the start that none of the characters in this drama is particularly admirable. The major players are King Minos of Crete; his queen, Pasiphaë; the god Neptune; Dædalus, a craftsman, tinkerer, putterer, and inventor, the original of the type; and a beautiful bull.
>
> The bull was bullish. King Minos was boastful, vain, and cruel. Pasiphaë was disrespectful of the gods and apparently driven by lustful thoughts. Neptune was, like the other gods, exceedingly jealous and apt to be vengeful. Dædalus, though he was a clever artificer, was also a murderer; he was so envious of rival artificers that when his nephew, Perdix, invented a saw—modeling it on the shape of a fish skeleton—Dædalus pushed him off a tower to his death.

King Minos often boasted that he was a favorite of the gods, that they listened with particular favor to his prayers, and that, therefore, he could obtain virtually anything he wanted by petitioning the appropriate god. Perhaps, down the long corridor of time, you seem to hear the snorts and snickers of skeptics in the king's audience when he made these assertions; apparently, Minos heard them, too. To silence them, Minos went into his act, calling upon Neptune in his prayers, beseeching the god to send him a bull, which he promised to sacrifice to Neptune as soon as the Cretan skeptics had been silenced.

Neptune delivered; the bull appeared. However, because the gods like to work in mysterious ways, it was no ordinary bull. It was an extraordinarily beautiful bull. (We may find the notion that a bull might be "extraordinarily beautiful" a bit hard to swallow in our enlightened times, but the Cretans seem to have had no trouble with it.) Minos was dumbstruck by the bull's beauty; so was Pasiphaë, as we shall see. Under the influence of the bull's beauty, Minos reneged on his deal with Neptune; he refused to sacrifice the animal. Neptune was not happy with this turn of events. Gods, as a rule, like obedience. They go for groveling and abasement. When promised a sacrifice, they expect a sacrifice. Minos's impudence did not sit well with Neptune, who determined to make Minos pay dearly for it. With a god's ingenuity, he infected the beautiful bull with a kind of madness, inducing in it a violent fury that made it intractable and unpredictable, like the crazy people one encounters in small towns, characters who may be quaint in their way but are subject to irrational outbursts of violence and are best avoided.

The bull was not the only earthly agent of Neptune's wrath. He infected Pasiphaë with a kind of madness, too, but a madness different from the bull's; in her case, it was an irresistible passion for the bull. We shall have more to say about this later.

Minos needed help. He called on Hercules, the ubiquitous hero of ancient myth, archetype of all the heroes you find in your comic books. Hercules caught the rampaging bull, subdued it, and took it away to Greece, riding it there, the myth tells us, through the waves. (That bit about riding the bull through the waves is a detail that, like so many of the details, large and small, we are asked to accept in these old myths, doesn't seem likely.)

However, Hercules's ridding Crete of the rampaging bull did not end Minos's troubles. During its time in Crete, the bull had managed to sire a child, and now that child, the Minotaur (that is, "Minos's bull"), was causing no end of trouble. The Minotaur was a monster with the head of a bull and the body of a man. It went about terrorizing the people of Crete as its father had, but did an even better job of it.

Again, Minos needed help. He turned to Dædalus, that famous artificer. Minos had long admired Dædalus's skills, but he had become less than fond of the man after Dædalus had abetted the love of Pasiphaë for the Minotaur's father, that extraordinarily beautiful bull that Neptune had sent in devious fulfillment of Minos's imprecations. In his hour of need, Minos seemed to set aside his animosity toward Dædalus, and the great artificer constructed for him a labyrinth, with passages and turnings winding in and about like the river Mæander. In this labyrinth he enclosed the Minotaur, which could not find its way out. Minos found that the labyrinth was also a fine place to imprison miscreants and foes, who became feed for the Minotaur that roamed the twisting passageways. In addition, after Dædalus had completed the labyrinth, Minos imprisoned Dædalus and his son, Icarus, there, for Minos's animosity toward Dædalus had never really waned and he hoped that imprisonment in the labyrinth would mean the end of Dædalus and his issue.

However, crafty Dædalus fashioned wings from feathers and wax so that he and Icarus could fly out of the labyrinth. Before they took to the air, Dædalus instructed Icarus in the use of the wings and the safety rules of the art of human flight as they were then understood. "Fly neither too high nor too low," he counseled his son, "but keep to the middle way." Well, you know how youngsters are: headstrong. Icarus took off, and in the manner of daredevil youth since time immemorial he soon scoffed at his father's advice, flouted his warnings, and stretched his wings. He flew too high, too near the sun, and the heat melted the wax that held the feathers in place. Without feathers, he was no longer a flyboy, merely a boy, and boys cannot stay airborne for long. Icarus fell into the sea and drowned. Let this be a lesson to you.

SOMETHING SEEMED TO BE MISSING from this story. The bull's child, the Minotaur, seemed to pop into it from nowhere, sired but un-born. The bull was the father, clearly, but who was the Minotaur's mother? The hints pointed to Pasiphaë. Could that be? Just imagine the storms raging in the teenage brains of Mrs. Fendreffer's charges upon hearing the phrase "abetted the love of Pasiphaë" for the extraordinarily beautiful bull. What on earth did that mean? We were young people eager for knowledge—or at least we were eager for knowledge in certain areas. Could a woman fall in love with a bull? Could a woman—ah—make love with a bull? How, precisely, would one abet such a love?

"Wait a minute, Mrs. Fendreffer."

"Yes, Bill?"

"You mean Pasi-whosis was in love with a bull?"

"Yes," Mrs. Fendreffer sighed, recognizing the opening wedge in a line of inquiry that she had endured every year for all of the thirty-nine that she had been teaching.

"Isn't that a little—" Bill, ordinarily forthcoming, hesitated and even seemed embarrassed.

"Yes?" prompted Mrs. Fendreffer.

"Perverted?" suggested Bill.

"Today I suppose we would call it a kind of bestiality," Mrs. Fendreffer conceded, "but the ancients had standards different from ours."

"Is that why you call it the golden age, because they were fornicating with bulls?" asked Rose O'Grady, known as Spike.

"I don't want to hear any language like that in my classroom."

"Hey, I don't want to hear any stories about women—and married women at that—consorting with bulls—or any other animals for that mat-ter—behind their husbands' backs," said Bill.

"You don't object to their consorting with bulls if their husbands con-sent?" asked Spike.

"Even that would be pretty sick."

"Mrs. Fendreffer, may I ask a serious question?" said Spike in a seri-ous tone of voice.

"Please."

"It says in the book that Dædalus 'abetted the love of Pasiphaë for the Minotaur's father, that extraordinarily beautiful bull.'"

"'Abetted the love of Pasiphaë for the Minotaur's father, that extraordinarily beautiful bull.' That is correct."

"How?"

"What?"

"How did he abet the love of Pasiphaë for the bull?"

"That I do not know," Mrs. Fendreffer claimed. "I have been teaching these myths for many years now, and I have consulted many sources for elucidation of their mysteries, but I have never found any commentator who explains just what we are to take *abet* to mean in this case."

None of us knew, then, that Mrs. Fendreffer's ingorance was feigned, that it was a part of her teaching technique. For thirty-nine years she had been claiming not to know how Dædalus might have abetted the love of Pasiphaë for the Cretan bull and, thereby, she had been inspiring her students to go beyond the pages of *Ancient Myths for Modern Youth* and try to find the answer on their own.

Several of us did, that very afternoon. In a group, with Spike in the lead, we trooped to the school library. There, after half an hour's work, we found some additional information, but not enough. We walked to the Babbington Public Library, where, after another half hour's work, we found a bit more information, but still not enough. It was Spike who voiced our common frustration and suspicions to the librarian: "Hey," she said to the woman behind the reference desk.

"Yes?"

"We're trying to answer a question about one of the Greek myths, and all the books we check don't give us the real inside dope."

"Mm," said the librarian.

"Are you hiding the good stuff somewhere?"

The librarian looked up from her work and over her glasses and down her nose at Spike. Slowly a smile formed on her face.

"Are you in Mrs. Fendreffer's class?" she asked.

"Yeah," said Spike. She seemed as surprised by the question as the rest of us were. "How did you know?"

"This happens every year," the librarian said, and then a look of concern crossed her face. "Usually it's a little earlier in the school year, though," she said. "Poor Mrs. Fendreffer must be slowing down." With a sigh and a shake of her head she led us to a locked bookcase.

In that case was a book called *Antique Scandals: The Mischief Behind the Myths.* We took it to a table nearby and, huddled around it, sought what we wanted to know. We found it, some of it, and in the bargain learned a lesson about making inferences from an incomplete text, since some of the essential words had been hidden under thick black ink, there but obscured, the way the precise answer to a calculation on a slide rule is hidden by the very cursor that marks its location. Perhaps creating the opportunity to learn the lesson of inference was the point of blacking out the revelatory words, or perhaps Mrs. Fendreffer and her collaborators in the library merely wanted to conceal from us what they thought we were too young to know. Over the years I have decided to prefer to believe that they wanted us to learn something, not that they wanted us not to learn something.

We studied the passage in silence, making our individual decisions about what was missing.

"Oh," said Spike after a while. "So that's it."

"Just what I thought," said Marvin.

The rest of us made similar assertions to the effect that our suspicions were now affirmed, but I, because I have never known when to keep my mouth shut, said, in a tone that hid none of the disappointment I felt, "I was hoping there would be diagrams." The others burst out laughing, the librarian shushed us in the time-honored manner, and my reputation as a humorist grew considerably.

I HAD EXPECTED DIAGRAMS because I knew that if the tale of Dædalus's abetting Pasiphaë's love for the bull had appeared in *Impractical Craftsman,* there would have been diagrams. Many a reader would have attempted to build a replica of the false cow that Dædalus built, the essential equipment for abetting the love of a queen for a bull. I have no doubt about that at all. My grandfathers probably would have made the attempt. If I'd thought I had the skill, I probably would have tried it myself. Of course I would have.

boasting of his special relationship with the gods annoyed Queen
Pasiphäe, because she did not believe in gods. Of all the gods that
she did not believe in, she particularly refused to believe in the
goddess Aphrodite. There was something about Aphrodite or perhaps about the idea of Aphrodite that really rubbed her the wrong
way. Let us be frank about this. In all probability, Pasiphäe en-
vied Aphrodite. She wanted to be worshipped and feared as Aphrodite was.

Pasiphäe declined to make offerings to Aphrodite; years passed
without her suffering any apparent ill effect from this neglect, so
she scoffed at the idea that such a "goddess" as Aphrodite even existed. Dædalus, who was a special friend of Pasiphäe's, warned her
that such loose talk might reach the ears of Aphrodite, but it was
too late. Aphrodite had heard Queen Pasiphäe's blasphemous
words and she planned revenge.

Now it was the case that, for reasons unknown, King Minos admired white bulls. You have to accept this as a given, or the rest of
the story makes no sense at all. Minos demanded that the world's
most magnificent white bull be brought to him. Lo and behold, the
bull was delivered. However, the bull had been sent by Aphrodite,
as part of her plot for revenge. No sooner had the bull arrived than
Queen Pasiphäe fell passionately in love with it. She confessed her
love to her dear friend Dædalus, and Dædalus felt deep sympathy
for the beautiful queen, so he abetted her passion by making a re-
markably realistic wooden cow, just big enough for Pasiphäe to fit
in, arranging her body in such a way that the bull would be able to
███████ her and thrust its ██████████ into Pasiphäe's ████████████
█████████████ Dædalus was a thoroughgoing, exacting craftsman, so
he finished the job by killing and skinning a cow and sewing its
skin around the wooden form as a covering. Pasiphäe climbed inside the false cow, and Dædalus wheeled it to the field where the
bull was wont to graze. When the bull arived at the field it seemed
to see a beautiful cow already there. Smitten and ████████ the bull
trotted to the wooden form, █████████it, and, thanks to Dædalus's
cunning artifice, ███████████with the eager Pasiphäe. After the usual
nine months, Queen Pasiphäe gave birth to the creature that became known as the Minotaur, since it had the head of a bull.

. . . some of the essential words had been hidden under thick black ink . . .

Chapter 10
A Source of Motivation

STRETCHED OUT along the bulkhead beside the estuarial reach of the Bolotomy River one morning, Raskol and I were daydreaming in tandem, trading ideas about the things we might be doing if the day were not the sort of lazy summer day that invites a boy to do nothing but loaf and daydream, when the subject of flying arose.

"The subject of flying arose." That isn't accurate. I realize, upon reflection, that it suggests a chance provocation, the possibility that a light plane buzzed overhead, introducing the subject, or perhaps some other provocation no less apt but less direct, like a bumblebee buzzing by, or a provocative something even less obvious, like the leisurely ascension of the morning mist from the slack surface of the river. To be truthful, as I am struggling to be in this full and frank disclosure, the subject did not simply arise: I injected it into the meandering conversation by recalling my ride in a floatplane.

On a day several summers earlier, I had flown in what was then called a "seaplane" and is now called a "floatplane" while on vacation with my parents and maternal grandparents in the mountains of New Hampshire. After I had made the flight, my first in a plane of any kind, I couldn't stop talking about it.

Allow me a moment here to explore my motives for wanting to talk about it, for wanting to tell others about the experience I had had, because I think I see in those motives the prototypes of my motives for writing my memoirs. In part I was trying to re-create the experience for myself in the telling; in part I was trying to "share the experience," to allow my listener the vicarious experience of it; in part I was trying to preserve the experience, enclose it in a protective layer of words, within which it would not fade or dim; and in part I was just bragging. None of my friends had flown, and I was, I understood, displaying my distinction every time I brought the subject up, every time I tried to describe for them the sensation of sitting in a light plane (actually, squatting, in a tight space without a seat behind the two seats where the pilot and my father sat), skimming across the water, and then rising slowly into the air.

I injected the subject of flying with this preamble: "It would be neat if we could see Babbington from the air, the way I saw Osopuco Lake and the town of West Burke when I—"

"When you rode in that seaplane," said Raskol with a stage yawn and a tone that indicated more than clearly that he had heard the seaplane story more often than he had wanted to hear it.

"Yeah," I said. I wasn't going to force the story on him. He and I were friends. I might have forced the story on a stranger, or on an acquaintance whose goodwill I would have been willing to risk for the satisfaction of reliving the adventure in the telling, but I wouldn't force it on a friend. I fell silent, waiting. Maybe a stranger or an expendable acquaintance would come by.

After a while, Raskol said, with the generosity of friendship, "That must have been a great ride."

"Yeah," I said, but without much enthusiasm, since I evidently wasn't going to get to tell him about it all over again.

He put his hands behind his head, with his fingers interlaced, closed his eyes, and said the kindest words a friend can say: "Tell me all about it."

I BEGAN SLOWLY, as if I were struggling to recover the memory for his benefit. "There weren't many planes up there," I said. "It's pretty far away from things, and it's not on the way to anywhere, so you don't see many planes in the sky, but a couple of times a day I'd hear a buzzing above me and I'd look up and find it there, turning in a wide arc before coming in for a landing. Or sometimes I'd happen to be looking out across the lake, just enjoying the view, and I'd see it taking off. Of course, I wanted to be in it. I wanted to take off in it, fly around in it, land

Fig. 155. A seaplane with two floats. This is the most common type of seaplane.

Luscombe Airplane Corporation

I had flown in what was then called a "seaplane" . . .

in it. Some people said that the pilot took hunters deep into the woods. Others said that he flew sick people to hospitals miles away. When I heard them say those things, I'd smile to myself, because they were the things that adults would say, and even think. They would think that a person had to have a reason for owning and flying a plane with pontoons."

"Fun would be enough of a reason, wouldn't it?"

"That's what I thought. Exactly what I thought."

"I guess that's where I got it. I must have heard you say it sometime."

"There was a tavern of some kind in the little town. I never saw it, but my parents and grandparents used to go there in the evenings to have a beer. I think the parents who were vacationing used it as a way of getting away from their kids."

"In a way, you could say that the kids used it as a way of getting the parents out of their hair," he interrupted.

"What?" I said, rattled by the interruption.

"Nothing. Sorry. Go on."

"Where was I?"

"In the tavern, where your parents met the pilot and persuaded him to take you for a ride in the seaplane."

"I told you that already?"

"Many times, but please tell it again. I keep forgetting the details."

"Well, they were having a beer at the tavern one night, and the bartender said something to the guy sitting next to them that made them think that he must be the guy who flew the seaplane, so they asked him if he was, and he said yes."

"Oh, yeah. That's it."

"They got to talking, and my father bought him a beer and told him that his son watched the plane with obvious longing whenever it flew overhead."

"Is that what your father said, 'obvious longing'?"

"That's what he said he said."

"He's smarter than he looks, your father."

"Maybe."

"No offense intended."

"None taken."

Chapter 11
In Search of Some Bits of Memory

I PAUSED in my reading, because I had come to the point in my account of the flight in the floatplane beyond which I was going to begin making things up. Albertine, because she is as much friend as lover, said, "Don't stop. Tell me all about it."

"I hardly remember it," I said truthfully.

"I hear the sadness in that."

"And I feel it. These memories fade, no matter how much we wish to hang on to them."

"Can't you poke and probe and bring it back?"

"I can poke and probe and bring something back, and then I can add to that whatever else comes drifting in on the wind, and out of what I actually remember and what comes drifting in I can make something that resembles a memory."

"Go ahead. I'd like to hear it."

"I don't think that it would belong in a full and frank disclosure."

"Excluding what comes drifting in would be hiding something, wouldn't it?"

"Are we going to chop a little logic here for my sake?"

"I think I'm going to argue that for you a remembered experience now consists not only of the memory but of the associations that cling to the memory—"

"Like the bits of cat fur that clung to my zwieback when I dropped it on my grandmother's kitchen floor."

"When you were an itty-bitty baby boy."

"Yes."

"Exactly what I mean, I think."

"I can't recall zwieback now without recalling the bits of cat fur stuck to it, and the cat, and the way the cat curled up beside my grandmother on her scratchy scarlet sofa, and the sofa itself, and on and on."

" 'The memories of childhood have no order, and no end.' "

"Yes, and I've come to think that the reason they have no end is that the man recalling the boy has a boundless capacity for invention."

"Try to curb that tendency, climb into that floatplane, and tell me what went on."

"Let's see. I remember a lot of aluminum, aluminum sheets, the panels of the doors, the floor. I remember being squeezed into the plane, behind the seats, but I don't really remember my squeezing in, the act of getting into the plane, or getting into place behind the seats. That memory is already confused with others, and with an image of a floatplane bobbing beside a dock from some movie or other. I think it's a movie called *Day of the Painter*. I do remember being behind the seats, in a tight space—"

"It wasn't a four-seater?"

"What?"

"It sounds as if you were squeezed in behind the pilot and your father."

"I was—I think."

"If the pilot flew hunters into the woods, I would think he'd have a plane with three seats available for passengers rather than just one."

"You're right! I was behind the second row of seats."

"Who was sitting in the second row?"

"My grandfather was on the left."

"And?"

"My grandmother was on the right."

"And your mother?"

"She didn't come along. She didn't want to. I'd forgotten that."

Chapter 12
I Seek a Little Help from My Friends

IN ONE OF MY GRANDFATHER'S old, yellowing issues of *Impractical Craftsman,* I came upon an article titled "Motorcycles of the Air." I read it with mounting excitement. This was no visionary, might-be, could-be, someday-in-the-distant-future article. The flying motorcycle, or aerocycle, that it described was built entirely out of things that I knew existed. All I needed was a motorcycle, fabric, tubing, and a few other things that an enterprising guy like me could find almost anywhere. This little airplane could be built. According to the article, it could be built in the family garage in a few weekends. "Could be built in the family garage in a few weekends": I still use that claim as a joke in my internal running commentary on the world. At that time, to me, a few weekends seemed a reasonable time for building a small plane. I calculated how many hours that might be. "A few," I reasoned, might mean four or five, six at the most. The amateur handyman couldn't be expected to put in more than eight hours a day on a weekend, after a week full of work or school, so the entire project ought to take less than a hundred hours to complete. If I got a friend to help me, we could do the job in fifty hours—not much more than one working week—and I had several friends who would be willing to help me with a project like this, not just one. With so many cooks in the family garage, I might be flying in a couple of days!

Impractical Craftsman offered a complete set of plans, full-scale. "Just roll them out on the garage floor, and you can assemble the aerocycle right on top of the drawings, ensuring that everything fits as it should—and ensuring that you don't leave anything out!" I could under-

In one of my grandfather's old, yellowing issues of *Impractical Craftsman* . . .

Motorcycles of the Air

TOOL BOX AND BATTERY COMPARTMENT

GAS AND
OIL TANKS

BRACING
WIRE

WING-TIP
AILERONS

ULTRA-LIGHT
TWO CYLINDER
AIR-COOLED MOTOR

WING TIP
AILERONS

LANDING
WIRE

DRAG
WIRE

SINGLE SPAR
WING BRACED
FORE AND AFT

BRACING
(FLYING) WIRE

CONTROL
CABLE

CENTRALLY
PIVOTED
CRUCIFORM
TAIL

SIDE RESTS ARE
LOWERED TO FORM
SUPPORT FOR SHIP
WHEN AT REST

AIRWHEEL

THE DREAM OF FLIGHT! We all have it, don't we? Doesn't it overcome you at times, reader? Your thoughts soar! Your heart takes wing! But you are rooted where you stand, earthbound and ponderous. When you see a raptor soaring on an updraft or a humble bumblebee lumbering by with a burden of pollen, don't you wish that you could take wing, too, and soar above the cares and woes that soak the dank earth in this vale of tears? All of us here at *IC* do—particularly around the end of the month, when your letters about the current issue begin drifting in, and we have to spend a sorry couple of days writing corrections and retractions and conferring with our attorneys. After that, some of us try to achieve the trick of levitation by imbibing copious quantities of "aviation fuel."

Many of you objected, some of you in terms that should not be employed between people who feel for one another a great mutual respect, and certainly not in letters sent through the U. S. Mail, that our visionary article on the anti-gravity Hovermobile was "unbuildable" and even "impossible to realize within our lifetime." Well, yes, but we here at *IC* think that some of you out there in Readerland were missing the point. That article was meant as inspiration, not as a blueprint for backyard homegarage builders. If we have inspired one young genius to begin the fundamental research into gravitation and motivation that will eventually lead him (or her!) to transform the Hovermobile from impossible to inevitable, then our article will have done its job.

Nonetheless, we do recognize that many of you were frustrated in your attempts to build Hovermobiles, and that some of you, if your letters are to be believed, spent many exhausting hours and expended considerable sums in the attempt.

Reader, our sole goal, desire, and ambition is to make your dreams come true. To that end, we present you with this exciting new project: the AEROCYCLE!

The above drawing shows details of an aerocycle plane as conceived and drawn by Douglas Rolfe, airplane expert. Ships of this type, though not yet commercially produced, have been made possible by recent development of new materials such as extremely strong but light metal alloys and light weight motors. "Flying scooters" like the one illustrated on this month's cover would not be practical for long-distance flying, but would be ideal for sports use. With the cost at a moderate figure, these aerocycles would very likely displace gliders in popularity. There are no novel departures from accepted airplane practice in these designs.

. . . I came upon an article titled "Motorcycles of the Air."

stand that working in that way was a good idea, but our garage didn't have a floor at that time, just a layer of sand, and the cost of the plans was not only more than I had to spend but more than I would have been willing to spend if I'd had it. Frankly, I scoffed at the idea that it was necessary to have the full-scale plans in order to complete the project successfully. They might be necessary for the plodding, literal-minded sort of builder who had to be told which way to turn each screw, but not for a clever kid with a good imagination. The pictures in the article ought to be enough for a start, and when in the course of building the aerocycle I got down to a detail that wasn't visible in the pictures, I could pause, think about it, and make a few drawings of my own to work it out before building it. The technique had worked for Leonardo. It ought to work for me.

I asked Margot and Martha Glynn to help, not so much because they were mechanically adept or interested in aviation but because they had listened tolerantly and often to my story of the seaplane ride and because it would be a treat to have them on the crew, a pleasure to watch them working in the tiny short-shorts they were wearing that year.

"Hmmm," said Margot. "This is not quite the sort of thing we enjoy doing, Peter."

"We're likely to get dirty doing this," said Martha.

"Yes," I said, "but you would look so good doing it."

"He has a point," said Martha.

"He does," said Margot, "but then we look good at almost everything we do, and this is just not for us. Sorry, Peter."

I asked Rose O'Grady, known as Spike.

"Wow," she said, looking at the article. "You're going to have to learn welding."

"I am?" I said. I hadn't counted on that.

"Sure," she said, giving me a friendly punch on the shoulder. "How else are you going to get all these steel tubes that form the support framework for the engine to stay together—wishful thinking?"

"Well—" I said noncommittally. (I had thought, if I could be said to have thought about it at all, that glue might work pretty well.)

A wistful expression came over Spike's face, a distant look into her eyes. "I always wanted to learn welding," she said.

"Now's your chance," I said.

"Yeah. Count me in." She gave me another punch. "Thanks, Pete."

I asked Marvin Jones.

He looked at the drawings and diagrams that accompanied the article. He looked at the drawings and diagrams that I had made. He brought his eyebrows together, furrowing the skin between them, and frowned.

"Anything the matter?" I asked.

"Was this designed by a trained aeronautical engineer?" he asked.

"Um—I don't know."

"And these pencil drawings, who did these?"

"I did," I said with what I thought was justified pride.

"I don't know much about aeronautics myself," he said, "but I think I know enough to say that this is not likely to get off the ground. If it does, it's going to be almost impossible to handle."

"Oh."

"You need a bigger tail surface, for one thing." He began reworking my sketch. "With a larger rudder—and ailerons—"

"So you'll help?" I said.

"Somebody's got to try to keep you from going down in flames," he said. "It might as well be me."

I asked Matthew Barber.

"Um—well—" he said. He fidgeted. He thrust his hands in his pockets. He frowned. He seemed to be stalling. He seemed embarrassed.

"Is there anything wrong?" I asked.

"Wrong? Of course not. What makes you ask that?"

"You're not answering me. You're stalling. You seem embarrassed."

"I—it's just that—I—"

"You don't want to help."

"I'll help."

"What is it, then?"

"Oh—it's just that—there's something I have to tell you. The guidance counseler—Mrs. Kippwagen—told me about a summer institute in math and physics—out in New Mexico—and she gave me a brochure about it—and I read through it and I said to myself, 'Peter would really enjoy this'—but I never told you about it—and I applied for it—and I got in—so I'm going to be going to New Mexico and studying advanced math and physics under the blazing sun—but I'm feeling completely miserable about it because I should have told you—"

"Hey, forget it," I said chivalrously. "I'll go see Mrs. Kippwagen and get an application—"

"It's too late," he said, and to his credit he hung his head in shame when he said it. "The deadline's passed."

Chapter 13
The QT-909, from QT Flying Machines

"IT'S AN AMAZING THING to say, an amazing thing to realize, but all of this makes me feel an almost overwhelming nostalgia—"

"You're sure you mean nostalgia?"

"I think so. I mean a yearning to return to an earlier experience, to experience again the sensations that I felt then, the springtime fervor and confidence I felt when I decided to build that plane, to see and hear again the responses of my friends, to stand once more on the sand floor in the family garage, even to listen again to Matthew's spluttering admission of his treachery—all of it."

"Nostalgia, you know, was originally perceived as a disease."

"I knew that."

"Of course you did."

"Wasn't it a disease of Belgian conscripts who were posted far from home and so fervently yearned to be back that they languished and died?"

"Something like that. It was originally identified by a Swiss physician, late in the seventeenth century."

"I bet you know who that Swiss physician was, don't you?"

"I'm afraid I do."

"Give, my sweet."

"He was Johannes Hofer, and he found evidence of the disease in Swiss living abroad who would rather not have been living abroad—young girls sent away to serve as domestics, for example, or soldiers fighting in foreign lands. They all felt the pain that accompanies intense and prolonged homesickness, a painful and debilitating desire to be back home again, and that is what Hofer called nostalgia, coining the term by combining the Greek *nostos,* meaning 'a return home,' and *algos,* meaning 'pain.'"

"You've got to cut back on those crossword puzzles."

"I'm thoroughly addicted. It's gone too far. There's nothing I can do about it now. So. Are you sure you're feeling nostalgic?"

"Maybe not, but I am feeling earthbound and ponderous. I'd like to take off."

"Shall we play hooky for the day?"

"It's more than that," I said, pouring coffee for me and tea for her. "This morning I am facing a workday full of annoying tasks that won't bring me any reward at all, not even the reward of feeling that I've done a job, because the job won't be done when the day is done. I'm going to have to work right through the weekend, and when the job is eventually done, in the small hours of Monday morning, I will not be satisfied with what I have done. All I will be is tired."

"I'm sorry for you," she said loyally.

"I know you are, and I am sorry for myself, very sorry for myself, and I know that that is immature and ignoble, but—"

"Yes?"

"Al, I really would like to have that aerocycle. My thoughts soar, but I am rooted here, earthbound and ponderous. You and I would get aboard, and we would fly away. We'd need an aerocycle built for two, of course."

"I should hope so."

"Al! Why don't we go? We could retrace my route to New Mexico."

"Well, (a) we don't have an aerocycle—"

"I could build one. Another one."

"Wait a minute. Are you serious?"

"I've been looking around the Web. Quite a few companies offer airplane kits for the home builder."

"Am I dreaming?"

"Just consider this one," I said, producing a printout that I had earlier kept concealed in the folds of the newspaper. "The QT-909."

"It looks like a coffin," she said. After a moment's further inspection, she added, "With wings," but not with the eagerness of one who hopes to climb aboard and soar above the quotidian cares of the workaday world.

"According to the people at QT Flying Machines, the kit is so complete and the directions are so clear that even a rank novice can assemble a 909 with ease—and I'm not a rank novice."

"How much does it cost?"

"The average QT-909 builder can be flying in less than two hundred eighty hours."

"'Can be.' How much does it cost?"

"The kit includes virtually everything one needs to build a 909."

"'Virtually.'"

"Well, everything except a few parts that you can find in almost any hardware store."

"'Almost.'"

"One of the remarkable things about the 909 is the fact that you can hitch it behind a car and tow it to the airport."

"Currently, the budget will not support the purchase of a car."

"The wings fold back against the sides of the fuselage—"

"Not while you're in the air, right?"

"Rarely, I'm sure."

"Why am I reminded of something made out of feathers and wax?"

"Mostly plywood, actually. Glued together with epoxy."

"You want to take your honey into the clouds in a plywood plane?"

"The 909 needs barely a hundred feet of takeoff roll before she slips the surly bonds."

"Impressive. How much does this plywood kit cost?"

"No more than that used roadster with the FOR SALE sign that you sigh over when you walk past it every morning."

"I suggest that you confine your flying to the realm of the science of imaginary solutions."

BALZAC WAS A MASTER of the science of imaginary solutions. In *Louis Lambert,* Balzac wrote, "Whenever I like, I can draw a veil over my eyes. Suddenly I go back into myself, and there I find a dark room, a *camera obscura,* in which all the accidents of nature reproduce themselves in a form far purer than the form in which they appeared to my external senses."

I sometimes draw that veil. I am not so adept that I can draw it whenever I like, but I can draw it at times. The place where I find the pure reproductions of the accidents of nature, my equivalent of Balzac's "dark room," is memory, of course, and even a painful memory is a refuge from a painful present. Perhaps, reader, you feel, as I do, that much of the present is not what you wish it were, not only your personal present but the present of our contentious, bullying species. Sometimes, I just want to fly away, to take flight, take off, make my getaway.

Flight! The word itself makes my thoughts soar, and saying it, softly, to myself, in a time of troubles, makes me feel a bit of its lift. Balzac has the young Louis Lambert say,

> Often have I made the most delightful voyage, floating on a word down the abyss of the past, like an insect embarked on a blade of grass tossing on the ripples of a stream. . . . What a fine book might be written of the life and adventures of a word! It has, of course, received various stamps from the occasions on which it has served its purpose; it has conveyed different ideas in different places; but is it not still grander to think of it under the three aspects of soul, body, and motion? Merely to regard it in the abstract, apart from its functions, its effects, and its influence, is enough to cast one into an ocean of meditations. Are not most words colored by the idea they represent? Then, to whose genius are they due?
>
> . . . Is it to this time-honored spirit that we owe the mysteries lying buried in every human word? In the word *true* do we not discern a certain imaginary rectitude? Does not the compact brevity of its sound suggest a vague image of chaste nudity and the simplicity of truth in all things? The syllable seems to me singularly crisp and fresh.
>
> . . . I chose the formula of an abstract idea on purpose, not wishing to illustrate the case by a word which should make it too obvious to the apprehension, as the word *flight* for instance, which is a direct appeal to the senses.

Perhaps you sometimes have, as I do, so strong a desire for flight, so strong a yearning to leave your present circumstances, that you are willing to trust your fate to feathers and wax. At such times, if I am able to, I draw a veil.

Chapter 14
No Laughing Matter

I AM ASTONISHED to realize how deeply I felt the sting of Matthew's treachery, and how deeply I feel it even now, so many years after the first stab. At the time it was like a sudden cramp, or the deep, sharp pain of a broken tooth, or a broken bone. Matthew was right in thinking that I would have wanted to go to the summer institute in math and physics. I wanted to go even after he had told me that going was impossible. Perhaps because I wasn't quite convinced that the deadline had passed, or perhaps because some perverse impulse to increase the pain of missing out compelled me, I visited Mrs. Kippwagen and asked to see the brochure that had lured Matthew to the program.

"I'm afraid it's too late to apply," she said.

"I know," I said. "Matthew told me, but I just want to see what I'm missing. Something in me won't be able to rest until I know what might have been."

She gave me the brochure, and then she added to it a useless application form. I stared at her, searching her face for any evidence of a smile.

"Mrs. Kippwagen," I said slowly, not quite sure whether I would actually ask her what I wanted to ask her.

"Yes?" she said, a bit warily.

"Why didn't you let me know about this in time to apply? I would have liked to go. I probably could have gotten in, if Matthew got in. My grades are better than his, especially in math and science, and I—"

"The feeling here," she said, tapping the eraser of her pencil on the blotter that covered most of the surface of her desk, "within the administration of the Babbington Public School System, was that only one student was likely to be chosen from any one town, and we wanted that student to be the best representative of the system we could put forth."

"That's Matthew?" I asked.

"We decided that it was Matthew," she said. The rhythm of the tapping pencil never altered.

I asked the classic question: "What's he got that I haven't got?"

"The right attitude," she said without half a moment's hesitation. "Matthew is a boy who exudes seriousness of purpose. People look at him and say to themselves, 'This is a sober boy, a boy who has put aside childish things, a boy who probably reads the world news every day and clucks his tongue over that chronicle of human misery—'"

"Mrs. Kippwagen," I asked, "are there any other summer institutes like this—maybe some that I could still apply for?"

"I've never heard of anything like this before," she said. "This is a new idea. It's a response to a national crisis. It's no laughing matter."

THE BROCHURE led off with these words:

YOUTH OF AMERICA! UNCLE SAM NEEDS YOU!

This is what followed:

Enemy Powers are training their youth to build rockets, satellites, and fearsome weapons.

Our intelligence tells us that their youth are far ahead of our youth. This means you!

We need a new generation of whiz kids who can build rockets, satellites, and fearsome weapons for us!

That's why Your Government, working through the privately funded Preparedness Foundation, is sponsoring the Summer Institute in Math, Physics, and Weaponry (SIMPaW) for promising high school students.

The Summer Institute is a six-week residential program for bright, serious high school students. (NOTE: For purposes of security and secrecy, the Institute is held on the campus of the New

Mexico College of Agriculture, Technology, and Pharmacy, and accepted students should refer to themselves as "future pharmacologists of America.")

As a student at the Summer Institute, you will pursue a challenging curriculum that will prepare you for the struggle that lies ahead.

Don't think that you'll be sitting in dusty classrooms studying empty theory! Oh, no! You'll get useful, practical experience in calculating missile trajectories and weapons yields.

Should You Apply?

The Summer Institute is not for everyone. We're not looking for sluggards, laggards, or dullards. If that's you, pass us by. No comedians, either, thank you. We're looking for boys (and girls) with *promise,* the ones who stand at, or near, the top of their class, do their homework, and take out the garbage. If that's you, Uncle Sam says, "I want you to fill out the application form."

You must submit the application, school transcript, signed loyalty oath, and letters of recommendation in triplicate by April 15. No application received after that date will be considered for any reason under any circumstances. (And don't try to blame a late application on the U. S. Mail. Nothing stays those loyal couriers from their appointed rounds, and we will look with double disfavor on the application of anyone who claims that something does.)

Despite the clear statement that no applications would be entertained after the deadline, I decided to make the effort anyway, in the never-say-die spirit of Dædalus. I completed the application. I arranged to have my transcript sent to the institute. I noticed that the application did not include the loyalty oath that was mentioned in the list of required documents; I considered this the application's equivalent of an exam's trick question and devised a loyalty oath of my own. I lined up letters of recommendation, and I wrote a heartfelt cover letter explaining why my application was late and all but begging to be considered after the deadline.

Dear Admissions Committee:

I am submitting an application for admission to the Summer Institute. I realize that this application will reach you after the official deadline for submission of applications, through no fault of the U. S. Mail. I trust that you will consider my application, despite its lateness, on the grounds that I have a good excuse for being late. Here it is: until now, no one had ever told me that there was such a thing as the Summer Institute.

I am convinced that attending the Institute is the very thing I need to advance me in my goal of becoming a pharmacologist, if you know what I mean. I have been serious about this goal since I was a young boy, and I have always done my homework on time. (Well, almost always. Nearly on time.) I have enclosed a signed loyalty oath. (None was supplied, so I wrote my own, which I sincerely hope will be acceptable.)

You should receive, under separate cover, my school transcript and letters of recommendation from my math and physics teachers and from a pharmacist in my home town of Babbington, New York.

I implore and beseech you to give my application full consideration despite its lateness. If, on a winter's night, a traveler arrived at your door late, when dinner was done and the lights were out, seeking shelter and the warmth of human companionship, would you turn him away? Of course not. Though he arrived late, you would throw your door open wide and welcome the weary applicant with hot soup, a warm fire, and a soft bed, wouldn't you? Isn't that the American way?

Sincerely yours,

Peter Leroy

Loyalty Oath

I hold these truths to be self-evident, that all men are created equal, that they are endowed by their creator with certain

unalienable rights, that among these are life, liberty, and the
pursuit of happiness—that to secure these rights, governments are
instituted among men, deriving their just powers from the consent
of the governed, that whenever any form of government becomes
destructive of these ends, it is the right of the people to alter or
abolish it, and to institute new government, laying its foundation
on such principles, and organizing its powers in such form, as to
them shall seem most likely to effect their safety and happiness.

   Peter Leroy

It didn't work. The admissions committee was not amused, and my
application was not entertained. I received a small slip of paper printed
with the following rejection notice:

Thank you for your interest in the Summer Institute. Your application was received after the Institute's deadline for receipt of applications had passed. Therefore, it cannot be considered. The Institute
wishes you the best of luck in your future endeavors.

Chapter 15
On Rejection's Gray Gloom

ALBERTINE CROSSED THE ROOM, rumpled my hair, sat beside me, and gave me a hug, responding as much to the sigh that I appended to my reading of the preceding chapter as to its text, I think.

"Were you horribly disappointed, my darling?" she asked.

"Yes, I was," I admitted. "I had forgotten this sad section of the tale, or perhaps I had chosen not to remember it. When that letter arrived, I fell into rejection's gray gloom."

"But you hadn't actually been rejected. Your application was late. It was never considered, not rejected."

"Try to tell an adolescent boy that there is a difference. Do you suppose that if he calls a girl and asks her to go with him to the first dance of the school year and hears her tell him that she already has a date, he allows himself to feel that he hasn't actually been rejected because his application was late and therefore could not be considered?"

"I see what you mean."

"Of course you do."

"He sinks into that gray gloom you mentioned just a moment ago."

"His estimation of his own self-worth slips lower and lower—"

"He asks himself why she couldn't invent some excuse to rid herself of the earlier bird and put him, the late applicant, in the place held by the earlier applicant and, ultimately, in the arms of the girl herself."

"Yes, I guess he does—"

"He tells himself that if she cared for him, she certainly would do that."

"Right—"

"He tells himself that if she *really* cared for him, she would never have accepted the invitation of any other applicant no matter how early the application was made."

"Yes, that too."

"He begins to wonder whether he shouldn't have done something to distinguish himself, to move himself to the head of the line of suitors, so that the timing of his invitation would not have been a factor in the girl's decision."

"I don't know about that—"

"He curses himself for not having offered to fly her to the dance in an airplane of his own construction."

"What?"

"That would have made her change the rules and accept him in place of the earlier applicant."

"Hey—"

"But no, no. Such thoughts would bring the fault too near himself, and the gray gloom of rejection is better than the bitter tea of inadequacy or incompetence or ineptitude, so he allows himself to slip a little lower, and a little lower, until he is sure that the girl wouldn't go to a dance with him if he were the last young aviator on earth, covered in glory, and he suspects that she would stay at home on the night of the dance, watching her parents play mah-jongg rather than be seen in public on his arm."

"I think I'll move on to the next chapter."

"Oh, goody."

Chapter 16
Mr. MacPherson Raises a Question

MY FRENCH TEACHER, Angus MacPherson, must have noticed the downcast look that I wore throughout his class—a particularly knotty one on the uses of the subjunctive—because he stopped me on my way out the door and said, with a look of concern, "Peter, you seem a bit—how do you put it—down in the dump."

"Dumps," I said.

"Yes, that's it, the dumps, 'down in the dumps.' But why should it be so? Here in Babbington there is but one dump, unless they are hiding another from me. Are they? Is there a dump known only to initiates in a secret society of refuse and rubbish?"

"Um, no," I said. "I don't think so."

"Then one must be down in the dump, not the dumps, and that is where you seem to be. Why is that, Peter?"

"I've been rejected," I said.

"Ah! An affair of the heart! Of such sweet pain the teenage years are full to overflowing, I am afraid. Doubtless you will experience rejection many times. 'Learn young, learn fair; learn auld, learn mair.' In my own case—"

"It was more like being rejected by a college."

"How time flies! 'There's nae birds this year in last year's nest.' Are you after leaving us for college already?"

"No. Not yet. But I was hoping to spend the summer in New Mexico at a summer institute for promising high school students."

"Ah. That's a lot to parse all at once. An institute, you say?"

"Yes."

"What would that be? Not an institution, certainly? Not a house for the mad, I hope?"

"No, no. It's just—I guess it's—well—I don't exactly know what it is. A kind of summer school."

"Glorified by the name of Institute. I see. For promising high school students, you said?"

"Yes."

"I'm fully familiar with high school students, after trying to teach them to conjugate irregular verbs these past eight and twenty years, but I'm a bit less certain about what *promising* might mean."

"I think it means students who show promise."

"Students who show promise? What do they promise, pray?"

So far as I know, the Socratic dialogue had not yet become a Method of Instruction in the pedagogical armamentarium of American education, as it was to become not many years later, but Mr. MacPherson was already a practitioner of it, a pioneer in his way.

"I guess they promise to get better—improve—do remarkable things."

"Do you consider yourself a promising student?"

"Yeah. I think I've got promise."

"You think that you are likely to do remarkable things?"

"Well—I hope so."

"'Him that lives on hope has a slim diet.' What do you hope to do that's in the remarkable class?"

"I—um—I don't know—I—"

"Not a promising beginning," he said.

"I'm going to build an airplane out of parts of old motorcycles," I asserted suddenly.

"Now that is a promise! I see that you are a promising lad after all. So, with your being such a promising lad, why did the Institute for Promising Lads not accept ye?"

"Oh—my application was late—and I didn't mention anything about building the airplane."

"Hmmm. I see. Well, 'nae great loss but there's some smaa 'vantage.' With the loss their having passed you over, the advantage is that you are, I suppose, available if other institutes come looking for recruits?"

"Sure—but—"

"Yes?"

"I'd like to go to one that's held in New Mexico. I've kind of got my heart set on going to New Mexico now."

"And 'where the heart yearns to go, we mun go or die in the attempt,'" he murmured, mostly to himself, while he began rummaging through some papers on his desk. "Let's see—I've got a notice from the Institute for Future Œnophiles—but that's in Paris—and there's the Institute for the Study of Callipygian Women—but that's on the island of Martinique—and—ah!—here's the Faustroll Institute of 'Pataphysics—in New Mexico."

"What?" I blurted hopefully.

He held a clutch of papers toward me. I snatched them from him and examined them. There was a notice from the administration about scheduling final exams, a list of lunch menus for the remainder of the school year, and a memo from the vice principal reminding faculty members that only he was permitted to park in the space beside the space allocated to the principal himself.

"Oh," I said, managing a smile. "It was a joke."

"Something to lift you out of the dump."

"You really had me going there."

"'Nane can play the fool sae well as a wise man.'"

"I guess so," I said on my way out the door.

"Peter," he said to my back, "ask yourself something."

"Yeah?"

"Does it really require an institute to get you to New Mexico?"

Chapter 17
Antinostalgia

THE ANSWER to Mr. MacPherson's question was, I decided while thinking about it on the way home, yes. Something as solid and convincing and worthy as the Summer Institute that Matthew would be attending would be required to justify my going to New Mexico—to justify it to my father, who retained full veto power over any travel that might take me farther than the next town. A trip to New Mexico was likely to cost some money, and if I was going to ask my father to contribute to the expenses—which was what I had in mind—I was going to have to be prepared to convince him that I was going in pursuit of something that he would approve, like an education at an institute sponsored by an agency of the United States government.

New Mexico. "Land of Enchantment." The slogan stared at me from a poster that I had tacked to the wall beside my bed. I had written to the Department of Tourism of the State of New Mexico and requested everything that they could send me. I'd received a large, fat envelope stuffed with maps, posters, guidebooks, and brochures. Any of it that was suitable for framing I had thumbtacked to the walls of my room, in the gaps between my maps. I was surrounded by New Mexico and potential routes to New Mexico, but I was stuck in Babbington; my mind was in the Land of Enchantment, but my physical self was in the Land of Disappointment. I had to find a way to get there—but how?

I summoned a council of friends. We met in a booth at Kap'n Klam, Porky White's clam bar.

"If only there were some other institute that I could get into," I said, concluding my opening remarks, "I'm sure my father would let me go. In fact, it's the kind of thing he'd be eager to have me do. But if I just told him that I wanted to build the aerocycle and fly to New Mexico for the hell of it, he'd never let me do it in a million years."

They sat in glum silence. They all lived in similar circumstances. I wonder how many dreams of going elsewhere were entertained in the adolescent heads hanging over root beer and Coffee-Toffee soda that afternoon. We all wanted to go somewhere, anywhere, anywhere beyond Babbington. We wanted to be broadened by travel. Broadening was what we expected from travel, an enlargement of experience, an inflation of our essential selves.

Our teachers were to blame for this expectation and our collective wanderlust. They couldn't stop talking about the broadening effect of travel. Each of them had been somewhere and could prove it. They had slides. They had snapshots and postcards. They had souvenirs. Whenever one of those school days arrived with something in the air that made sitting in a classroom almost unbearable, we could mitigate the annoyance of our having to remain in school simply by asking about their travels.

Take, for example, Mrs. Bond. "Mrs. Bond, when you were in Minnesota, Land of 10,000 Lakes, did you find that—" one might begin, and following that prelude anything at all might be appended, and whatever it was it would induce in Mrs. Bond—who is serving here as a representative of all her colleagues, you understand—a reflective pause, bringing a recollective distance into her eyes, and sending her into what might be called a state of antinostalgia, the pain not of a yearning to return home but of a yearning to get away from home, or to return to a place other than home where one had felt for a while more keenly alive than one did at home, which, for Mrs. Bond, was more specifically the disease of Minnesotalgia, the yearning to be back in the Land of 10,000 Lakes rather than suffering the daily durance vile of teaching the history of New York State to some of its denser young citizens and spending her evenings in the smothering presence of Mr. Bond, who liked to think of himself as a humorist, the Man of 10,000 Jokes.

"Apply to the Faustroll Institute," said Matthew quietly.

"There isn't any Faustroll Institute," I said. "I told you—"

"Your father doesn't know that," he said, just as quietly.

Reader, I wish you had been there. I wish you could have seen those young heads rise, buoyed by the possibilities that Matthew had placed before us.

"Oh, this is going to be good," said Spike. She had a luminous smile, and she gave it to us now, allowing it to emerge slowly, to warm us, to drive away the chill drizzle of disappointment. "Very, very good."

"We'll need a brochure—" I said.

"It could just be an announcement," said Raskol. "If it's on official stationery, it wouldn't have to be a brochure."

"Then we'll need official stationery."

"I can do that," said Marvin. "I can make a linocut based on the seal at the top of the letter Matthew got, set some type, and run off a few sheets in the print shop."

"We'll need an application form—"

"We'll copy the one for SIMPaW," said Matthew.

"Don't forget to change the due date," Marvin cautioned him.

"And I'm going to have to get Mr. MacPherson to tell me what the Faustroll Institute of 'Pataphysics is supposed to be," I said.

Chapter 18
I Am Challenged

ALBERTINE FROWNED. She rarely frowns. When she does, my world churns.

"Don't you think that perhaps you're being too hard on him?" she asked softly.

"Mr. MacPherson?"

"No. Your father."

"Too hard on him?"

"You're making him into the grand naysayer, the crusher of all dreams, a comic-book villain. It seems a bit much to me."

"Have I never told you about the time when I was given the opportunity to see a play, in New York, a professional production, in a real theater, for the first time in my little life?"

"You have."

"I'll tell you again. These memories are so sweet. I love revisiting them. My father, the Grand Naysayer himself—"

"That's enough. I know the story. He wouldn't let you go. He made you paint the garage."

"Right."

"You've resented it ever since."

"Right."

"I just wonder sometimes if you have done the difficult work of getting inside his mind to find out what he wanted out of life, out of his life, what he might have yearned for."

I said nothing for a while. I went to the living room window and looked out over East 89th Street. Across the way, on the roof of a town house, one of our neighbors had set up a telescope and invited friends to view Mars during its extraordinary perihelic opposition. Host and friends were behaving in the cocktail-party manner, drinking drinks, eating snacks, and chatting, but one by one each of them would bend to the eyepiece of the telescope and peer through it, and I found that I could easily imagine that for some of them, the ones whose expressions altered while they were looking at the planet that had drawn so near but was still so far, the experience was broadening. They came away from the telescope silent and distant. They had been away for a while. They weren't quite back.

"It's not nostalgia that sends me back to where I've been," I said, turning toward Albertine, who had been reading while she waited for me to return. "It's curiosity. I want to notice what I didn't notice."

"Well, then, in that case—"

"Yes. In that case, you're right. Completely right. I ought to spend some time in my father's mind."

"I agree, but I think I'm going to be sorry that I brought it up."

I BEGAN TO WONDER. I began to wonder whether my father might have wanted many of the things that I had wanted myself. I began to employ the techniques that I learned during that summer I spent at the Faustroll Institute, the methods of the science of imaginary investigations, and some of my discoveries have found their way into the pages that follow.

Chapter 19
A Baedeker for a Wild Goose

I WAITED until Mr. MacPherson was alone. I stood outside his class-room, watching through the narrow window beside the door. He was con-jugating some esoteric verbs for half a dozen students, who were wearing the black berets and ribbons that identified them as members of the French Club, the *Coterie Française*. When they filed out at last, I knocked on the open door.

"*Oui?*" he said, still in the *Coterie* frame of mind.

"Mr. MacPherson, I have a question for you."

"Yes?" he asked, since it was only me.

"When you were trying to lift me out of the dump, with that joke about the Faustroll Institute—"

"The Faustroll Institute of 'Pataphysics."

"Right."

"Yes?"

"What made you pick that?"

"Pick that? What do you mean by 'Pick that'?"

"I mean, why did you make that up? The Faustroll Institute. Did you just pull that out of thin air, or is there something like it? Is it—by any chance—based on something real?"

"Ah. I see what you are asking. You are wondering, where do we get our ideas? When we have a burst of creative inspiration, where does it come from? Is it stimulated by something real—that is, as you put it, 'based on something real'—or does it come from 'nowhere,' so to speak? Is there a place within the mind called the imagination where nothing real

resides, a place that holds only things that are imaginary, or is the relationship between the real and the imaginary a more intimate one, with a
great deal of easy travel between the realm of the real and the realm of the
imaginary, no passport required, no entry or exit visa demanded, come
and go as you will—"

"I just want to know whether there is anything like the Faustroll Institute or whether I'm going to have to make the whole thing up from
scratch."

"'From scratch.' Why do we say that?"

"I don't know," I said. "It means 'from nothing'—"

"Not quite, I think. More likely it means 'from raw ingredients,' like
'from whole cloth.'"

"I guess—"

"Perhaps you'll inquire about that at the Faustroll Institute."

"The Faustroll Institute, that's what I—"

"If they set you the task of writing a dissertation, perhaps you'll
choose to do it on the question of whether an imaginary solution can be
built from scratch, from whole cloth, or must needs be built from a kit, a
set of precut pieces—pieces that we cut as we live, without even noticing
that we're doing the work, and stack away in a cabinet, where perhaps
they grow dry and dusty with time, until the day when we find that we
need them, take them out, and assemble them to make a flying machine or
the underpinnings for a château in the Pyrenees."

"Sure. Okay. I don't know what you're talking about, but I'll do it if
I'm given the chance. What I need to know now is—"

"You need to know that 'pataphysics is the science of imaginary solutions, which symbolically attributes the properties of objects, described
by their virtuality, to their lineaments."

"Oh."

"Do you see what I'm saying, lad?"

"No."

"It's all in here." He opened a drawer of his desk, the top right-hand
drawer, which, for a right-handed person, is the drawer in which are kept
the things that are most frequently used—like a stapler—or the things that
one wants near at hand in a crisis—like a revolver. From the drawer he
took a small book. He handed it to me. It was *Gestes & Opinions du Doc-*

teur Faustroll, by Alfred Jarry, described in its subtitle as a *"roman néo-scientifique."*

"It's in French," I said.

"Sharp lad. If you want me to write you a recommendation for the Faustroll Institute, I'll need to see a translation of the first chapter."

"Oh."

"Shall we say tomorrow?"

"I guess."

"If you bring me a complete translation at the end of the summer, or at the start of the school year, I'll move you up to French IV."

"I'll try," I said, flipping through it.

"And if you bring me several translations, each different from the others, I'll put you in the advanced-placement class."

"But what about the Faustroll Institute?" I asked, almost pleading, almost whining.

"If you set out from here and go looking for it, with this book as your Baedeker and *vade mecum,* I'm sure that you will find the Faustroll Institute and perhaps even get to know the great Dr. Faustroll himself."

"You make it sound like Neverland, or Oz," I said, with the growing suspicion that he was having more fun with me than I ought to allow.

"Go to New Mexico. Take the book with you. Translate it as you go. See what you find."

"But I don't even really know what I'm looking for."

"'Seek till ye find, and ye'll never loss yer labour.'"

"Well—if it gets me to the Land of Enchantment—I'll do it—but it feels like a wild-goose chase."

"Now why in the world do we use that expression, apparently attributing to wild geese an aimlessness that surely isn't evident from their methodical migrations?"

Chapter 20
A Father-and-Son Conspiracy

MY MOTHER was easy to please; that is, I could please her easily. All I had to do was do something—and almost anything would do. She was ready to approve very nearly anything I did. She always expected the result to be something that would enhance my reputation and my résumé and make the world see my merits at last, which put her in marked contrast to my father, who, it seemed to me, expected most of my undertakings to turn into the sort of black mark that one did not want on one's permanent record.

"Peter's going to learn welding," my mother announced at dinner, flushed with the rosy prospects that this presented.

"Is that right?" said my father.

"I've already started," I said. "I got a free welding instruction book. I've been reading it."

"I always wanted to learn welding," my father said, and as he said it a wistfulness came into his voice that, to the best of my recollection, I had never heard before.

"Really?"

"Yeah. In my day, a guy who could weld, really weld, was sure to be popular."

"Is that true, Mom?"

"Oh, yes," she said. "I remember one boy in particular, Darren—"

"Darren," growled my father, evidently feeling the pain of an old wound. "What kind of guy is named Darren?"

"A guy who could weld," said my mother with a directness that made my father grunt and bend to his American chop suey. "Darren Smith. He had the most amazing hands," she recalled, extending her own and examining them. "They were large and sinewy."

"Darren Smith, 'a mighty man was he, with large and sinewy hands,'" I quoted.

"That's right," she said. "How did you know?"

"Just a guess," I said.

"His hands were so strong—and yet so fine—and in a way delicate—like the hands of a pianist."

I risked a sidelong glance at my father. He seemed angry. I might have said to myself that he seemed angry, as usual. I might have taken some cheap pleasure in the discomfiture that my mother's memory of Darren the welder had caused him. However, something—who can say what?—made me see him differently. Instead of anger, I saw disappointment. I saw that he really had wanted to learn welding. He had wanted to be popular. He might have wished, now, that some woman who had once been a girl when he was a boy might be recalling his capable hands.

"I'll lend you the free welding instruction book, if you like," I said.

He grunted.

"It's never too late," I added with the wisdom of fourteen.

Having said it, I immediately regretted what I'd said, realized that it was presumptuous of the son to counsel the father, and feared that I'd be belittled for it, but my father began to nod his head, slowly, then turned to me, and, with a smile that would have been invisible beside Spike's but lit our little dining room with unusual fluorescence, said, "You're right. Thanks. I'd like to take a look at it."

Obviously there would never be a better time for me to announce that I'd been accepted at the Faustroll Institute.

"I've got exciting news," I said.

"*More* exciting news?" said my mother.

"Much more exciting," I said. "I've been accepted at the Faustroll Institute for Promising High School Students."

"Oh, my goodness!"

"Promising?" asked my father.

"Yes. Showing promise. Likely to do remarkable things. That's me.

I've got promise. It's official. The Faustroll admissions committee has decided that I show promise. I'm in."

I put the forgeries on the table. When I had met with Matthew and Marvin and first seen what they had produced, I had been more than impressed. The package seemed solid enough, full enough, and well enough executed to fool anyone. Now, when it actually had to fool my father, I was suddenly not so sure.

"Oh, Peter. This is wonderful," said my mother. "I can't wait to tell the neighbors."

"It's in New Mexico," I added, by the way, "and I'm thinking of flying out there—"

"Flying!"

"—after I build an aerocycle."

My father, nobody's fool after all, looked at me for a long moment, and then we exchanged two things we had never exchanged before: one wink and one grin.

"I always wanted to learn welding," my father said. . . . "In my day, a guy who could weld, really weld, was sure to be popular."

Chapter 21
Employing the Power of Experimental Thinking, I Prepare to Weld

A finite universe is unimaginable, inconceivable. An infinite universe is unimaginable, inconceivable. Doubtless the universe is neither finite nor infinite, since the finite and the infinite are only man's ways of thinking about it; in any case, that finiteness and infiniteness should only be ways of thinking and speaking is also something inconceivable, unimaginable. We cannot take a single step beyond our own impotence; outside those walls, I feel sick and giddy. If the wall is no longer there, the gulf opens at my feet and I am seized with dizziness.

Eugene Ionesco, *Fragments of a Journal*

THE FREE WELDING INSTRUCTION BOOK was actually something less than a book, barely a booklet, but in the space of its few pages it managed to be extremely discouraging. Welding, I discovered as I read, could not be accomplished with the tools and equipment I already had or with supplies I might find around the house. Knowledge, skill, and large, sinewy hands were not sufficient to the craft of welding—not that I had large, sinewy hands, but had I had them, they would not have been enough. Equipment was required: tanks, torches, an eyeshield, gases, gloves, and a cart to lug all the gear from place to place. All of this equipment, the book announced every time a piece of it was mentioned, could be purchased from Dædalus Welding, and there was a handy order form in the back of the book.

I couldn't afford any of the equipment or supplies, and I doubted that my father could afford any of it either, so I began to fear for my prospects as a welder and, welding being apparently prerequisite to the construction of an aerocycle, my prospects as an aviator, a sojourner in the Land of Enchantment, and student of the Faustroll Institute. However, hope has always come as easily to me as despair, so, by reading the book carefully and thoroughly and by performing the welding exercises in my mind, as thought experiments, I prepared myself for the unlikely but not impossible event of my coming into some welding equipment through the agency of some sponsor, mentor, or angel as yet unmet.

Permit me an aside on thought experiments.

According to the *Stanford Encyclopedia of Philosophy,* thought experiments are "devices of the imagination," employed when "a real experiment . . . is impossible for physical, technological, or just plain practical reasons." The author of the encyclopedia article, James R. Brown of the Department of Philosophy at the University of Toronto, asserts that the "main point" of interest about thought experiments for a philosopher "is that we seem able to get a grip on nature just by thinking. . . . We visualize some situation; we carry out an operation; we see what happens."

Among the famous thought experiments that he cites are Maxwell's demon, Schrödinger's cat, and, "one of the most beautiful early examples," Lucretius's lance. My copy of Lucretius's *De Rerum Natura,* in W. H. D. Rouse's translation, being ready to hand, I am able to insert here the relevant passage:

> The universe then is not limited along any of its paths; for if so it ought to have an extremity. Again, clearly nothing can have an extremity unless there be something beyond to bound it, so that something can be seen, beyond which our sense can follow the object no further. Now since we must confess that there is nothing beyond the sum of things, it has no extremity, and therefore it is without end or limit. Nor does it matter in which of its quarters you stand: so true is it that, whatever place anyone occupies, he leaves the whole equally infinite in every direction.

Besides, if all the existing space be granted for the moment to be finite, suppose someone proceeded to the very extremest edge and cast a flying lance, do you prefer that the lance forcibly thrown goes whither it was sent and flies afar, or do you think that anything can hinder and obstruct it? For you must confess and accept one of the two; but each of them shuts you off from all escape, and compels you to own that the universe stretches without end. For whether there is something to hinder and keep it from going whither it is sent and from fixing itself at its mark, or whether it passes out, that was no boundary whence it was sped. In this way I shall go after you, and wherever you place your extremest edge, I shall ask what at last happens to the lance. The effect will be that no boundary can exist anywhere and the possibility of flight will ever put off escape.

Among the many fascinating things about that passage is the image at the end of it of Lucretius harrassing his reader, his opponent in the argument over whether the universe has a limit, driving him to the extremity, that is to say, to whatever, wherever, the reader has presumed the extremity to be, and annoying him so persistently with his badgering and yammering that the reader is urged or forced to flee ever farther, and the fact that the reader can keep fleeing Lucretius is the refutation of the reader's argument that there is a boundary beyond which he cannot go, the border of a land that none of us may ever enter. Is it only me, or do you also hear a plaintive moan under the triumphant tone of that ending sentence? "I'm right! Fly, fly, fly as far as you can possibly fly, but you can never escape. There is no way out of here, reader, none. I wish there were, but there is not. There is no escape."

Lucretius's thought experiment was popular in my set when I was a boy. I don't mean to suggest that any of us had read Lucretius or had the slightest idea who Lucretius was or that any of us had ever thought his way to the distant reaches of space with an argumentative companion and watched while the unnamed someone who had accompanied him cast a flying lance; I mean only that we rode third-class on the same train of thought. On nights when we lay in someone's back yard looking at the stars and exploring the limits of our little minds, we asked ourselves and one another, again and again, what was at the end of the universe. Every time we asked we concluded, as Lucretius had when he was out in his back yard with the argumentative lancer, that there was no end.

"You ever ask yourself what's at the end of the universe?" someone would ask, even if the question had been asked not so long ago, on another night.

"Yeah."

"I mean, what could be there? A brick wall?"

"Search me."

"Because if there's a brick wall, then what's on the other side of the wall? You know what I mean?"

"Yeah."

We would continue in this manner until we were at our wits' end, though we never reached the universe's. The little philosopher in these exchanges may not have been doing a very good job of playing Lucretius, but I suspect that the respondent was a lot like the lance-caster, and together they were working their way toward the age of reason.

It is not difficult to gain some faint idea of the immensity of space in which this and all the other worlds are suspended, if we follow a progression of ideas. When we think of the size or dimensions of a room, our ideas limit themselves to the walls, and there they stop. But when our eye, or our imagination, darts into space, that is, when it looks upward into what we call the open air, we cannot conceive any walls or boundaries it can have; and if for the sake of resting our ideas, we suppose a boundary, the question immediately renews itself, and asks, what is beyond that next boundary? and in the same manner, what is beyond the next boundary? and so on, till the fatigued imagination returns and says, there is no end.

Thomas Paine, *The Age of Reason, Part One*

Chapter 22
To Hell with Welding

WELDING seemed to stand in my way like a schoolyard bully blocking the water fountain, and I will admit that for a time I thought of abandoning the entire project and resigning myself to spending the summer in Babbington, but my friend Raskol salvaged my hopes and dreams by making welding not only unnecessary but useless.

One day he found me studying *Impractical Craftsman* during study hall (engaged, I thought then and think now, in an activity entirely appropriate for study hall, but one that was forbidden, since *study* was constrained to mean "doing work assigned in a course taught at Babbington High School," and if one was found to be engaged in any other pursuit — writing a love letter, reading a magazine, trying to calculate the size of the universe, or making mechanical drawings of a single-seat airplane — then the product and any attendant supplies or materials were subject to confiscation and, theoretically at least, destruction). I was studying the drawings of the aerocycle and sketching its structural skeleton. I had known that this sketching would be necessary, since the article did not include a plan for the skeleton, and I had expected it to be tedious and annoying, but it was turning out to be fascinating and puzzling. From the pictures in the article, I was trying to make working plans, translating the pictures, neither of which showed the craft with its skin off, into the type of three-view drawing we had been taught to make in shop class, where our drawings were limited to much simpler projects, such as, in my case, a wrought-iron armature to hold a plaque that read LEROY, which when it was finished I nailed with pride to one of the pillars that supported the roof over the front porch of the family home, and a wooden box that held and hid the cardboard box that Sneezles tissues were packed in, still allowing them to pop up one at a time when the projecting tissue was tugged, which my mother had installed in the bathroom, on the back of the toilet, on top of the tank.

"Are these the plans for the aerocycle?" Raskol asked.

At the time, I assumed that he must have mistaken my handmade, pencil-drawn plans for a commercial product, an assumption that, I realize now, may have been wrong.

"Yes," I said, "but not the plans that *Impractical Craftsman* sells. I haven't ordered those. They're too expensive. I'm trying to make my own plans based on the pictures in the article."

He bent over the plans and studied them closely. "Is this why you're going to learn how to weld?" he asked.

"That's right," I said, though my learning to weld was becoming less and less likely.

"Are you nuts?"

"Why do you ask that?"

"If you make this thing out of welded steel, it's not going to get off the ground. Never. Not a chance. It's going to be much too heavy."

"You're sure?" I asked hopefully.

"Sure. You've got to make this out of aluminum."

"Oh."

"It's light but strong."

"Sure."

"But you can't weld aluminum."

"Oh?" I asked, brightening.

"Well, I guess, theoretically, somebody could weld aluminum, but it would be a real bitch, what with aluminum's high thermal conductivity and low melting point. I wouldn't bother trying if I were you."

"What should I—"

"You've got to rivet it together."

"Oh." I was going to have to learn riveting. Did I sigh? Probably. Did I frown? Almost certainly. Riveting sounded as arcane, difficult, and expensive as welding. I think I recall that I began to consider flying to New Mexico on a commercial airliner, as Matthew would be doing. His ex-

penses would be paid by the Preparedness Foundation, and he would enjoy tasty meals served by smiling stewardesses, whose attentions were,
among my friends, none of whom had ever flown, legendary.

"Or—" said Raskol, with the impish grin of a person bearing good
news, "you can just drill the parts and bolt them together."

Perfect. Not only was drilling already within my repertoire of skills,
but my grandfathers owned jars and jars of nuts and bolts. I'd been playing with them since before I could walk. I could drill as well as the next
guy, and I could bolt far better than most. To hell with welding.

That afternoon, I began scavenging Babbington for aluminum. I was
astonished to find how much aluminum was going to waste in garages
and attics: tent poles, flagpoles, folding clothes poles and outdoor drying
racks constructed like umbrellas, folding chairs for lawn or beach, the
legs and tops of folding tables, the pylons from beach umbrellas, and even
window mullions and frames.

I want to take this opportunity to thank the citizens of Babbington for
contributing their scrap to my dream. My heart soared when my friends
and acquaintances, and even a few of my enemies, endorsed that dream
by donating some of the raw materials that would make it a reality. My
call for assistance sparked such a remarkable response, an outpouring of
aluminum, that it resembled a movement. Its adherents and workers were
zealous, some of them wrenching aluminum from the arthritic hands of
their reluctant grandparents, and the most fanatical of them resorting to
stealing.

I will confess to a heady feeling of power when I saw what I had unleashed—followed by a deflating feeling of impotence when I discovered
how difficult is the task of leashing a movement once unleashed. Aluminum scrap kept showing up at our house for years. Eventually the flow
dropped to a trickle, but the idea that I needed aluminum was still alive in
the world even after I had left Babbington for college, and my mother
would often finish her letters to me with a postscript laconically listing
the recent deliveries, such as: "P. S. two folding chairs and a tray today."

Chapter 23
Pinch-a-Penny, the People's Plane

ALBERTINE STARTLED ME. I had been lost in thought. (If Mr. MacPherson were here, he would ask me why I use that expression. In this case, I could tell him that I have often marveled at how apt it is as a description of my state when I am thinking in the experimental mode. I begin somewhere, with an idea or a question, and from that starting point I begin to wander. I go where my thoughts take me, and that is why Albertine has decided that I should no longer drive unless she is with me to bring me, when necessary, back from the distant place to which my thoughts have flown into the immediate context through which the car is hurtling. Sometimes she gives me a nudge to bring me back; sometimes she screams.)

She was looking over my shoulder. I was looking at my computer screen.

"What's that?" she asked.

"It's Pinch-a-Penny, the People's Plane," I said.

"Ah. The People's Plane."

"Anyone can fly it. You don't need a license. It democratizes flight."

"Anarchizes flight, you mean. Driving is bad enough, but just imagine 'anyone' getting into one of these things and whizzing around without training, tutelage, examination, or certification."

"Scary," I admitted. I pointed to the photograph. "I would like to point out, however, that the frame is made of aluminum tubing."

"It looks like a folding table."

"There are remarkable similarities between this plane and the one that I built—the resemblance to a folding table being only one of them."

"Did it really look like this?"

"The frame did—part of it—but by the time I was finished, I had made many original contributions to the design—"

"Improvements?"

"Adaptations inspired by necessity."

"Necessity being defined as the demands of aeronautical engineering and fluid dynamics?"

"Necessity being defined by what I had on hand," I muttered, returning to my study of the Pinch-a-Penny.

"Come on," she urged, with a nudge of her hip. "Tell me about the People's Plane."

"Well, Norton Prysock—"

"Norton Prysock? Who's he?"

"The designer of the Pinch-a-Penny."

"Nort to his intimates, no doubt."

"Well, *I* certainly wouldn't doubt it. Nort says here on his website that this plane can be built in about two hundred fifty hours, using only simple hand tools. Anyone can do it, just by following the steps in the construction manual and referring to the detailed plans."

"'Anyone,' says Nort."

"Says Nort."

"An unsupportable claim, I think. 'Anyone'? You would think that 'anyone' could make a decent bagel just by following the steps in the manual and referring to the detailed plans, but experience belies it again and again."

"He makes a point of the fact that no welding is required."

"The bagel analogy holds."

"He says he's sold more than two thousand sets of plans."

"I smell a home business for you there."

"Hundreds of Pinch-a-Pennies are currently under construction," I went on.

"Says Nort."

"Says he."

"I take that to mean that hundreds of Pinch-a-Penny projects are languishing in back yards and garages."

"Seven are flying. Have flown."

"Seven." She leaned toward the screen. "Tell me what you see here," she said.

I looked at the photograph on the Pinch-a-Penny website.

"I see a stocky man, whom I take to be Norton Prysock, standing beside what I assume is his own Pinch-a-Penny, at the point in its construction when it was complete except that the fabric that would eventually cover the wings, control surfaces, and, optionally, the fuselage aft of the cockpit had not yet been applied."

"Do we know that he ever did get around to covering the thing?"

"Skeptic," I whined.

"And daughter of a skeptic," she reminded me. "What did my father always say?"

"'Assume nothing.'"

"Look behind Nort and the Pinch-a-Penny, Peter, and tell me what you see there."

"There's an outbuilding of some kind, a shed or garage, or a shed with a carport attached—"

"—and the siding has never been put on it, just the raw boards that are supposed to underlie the siding."

"Right."

"And the roof has been covered with tar paper but not shingled."

"Right."

"There is a stack of something on the left and a stack of something else on the right, both stacks covered with tarpaulins."

"Maybe he's going to use those tarps as fabric for the wings."

"I wouldn't be surprised. And then whatever is under those tarps will be exposed to the weather, and in time will molder and rot."

"Maybe."

"Nort has a serious personality flaw, Peter. He is not a finisher. He probably abandoned the carport project when the Pinch-a-Penny passion struck."

"I don't know about that. He looks so relaxed and self-confident—the way he's leaning on the plane—" In the photograph, Nort was resting his right elbow on the aluminum just ahead of the cockpit.

"He *appears* to be leaning on it," said Albertine, "but I don't think he actually is."

"You don't?"

"No. There is a tension in his body that makes me think he is holding himself in that position, giving the appearance of the builder at his ease, resting on the plane he has built, but in fact being careful not to put any weight on it."

I looked more closely. I took the magnifying glass from my desk drawer and looked more closely still.

"Well?" she asked.

"You may be right," I said.

Chapter 24
Surplus Motorcycles? Why Not?

THE HEART of the aerocycle design was a surplus motorcycle. The people at *Impractical Craftsman* asserted that the builder could obtain a surplus motorcycle locally and easily. They passed over the acquisition of a surplus motorcycle so quickly, in so few words, that I got the impression of a vast glut of surplus motorcycles, a buyer's market in surplus motorcycles, and I was amazed that I hadn't ever seen any abandoned by the side of the road, considering that the glut must have made them all but worthless.

I looked in the Yellow Pages under "Motorcycles, Surplus," but there was no entry for "Motorcycles, Surplus." I looked under "Surplus," but the only listing there was for the Babbington Army and Navy Store, and I knew from my frequent visits that although they carried lots of useful gear, they had no motorcycles.

"Where are all the surplus motorcycles?" I asked my friend Raskol, who, I assumed, was likely to know.

"Surplus motorcycles?"

"Yeah. Aren't there a lot of surplus motorcycles going begging?"

"What makes you think that?"

"I got the impression—"

"—the misimpression."

"I don't think so."

"Hey, Ernie!" he called into the house.

"Whaddaya want, shithead?" growled one or the other of his brothers, both of whom were named Ernie, possibly because Raskol's parents were twice as fond of the name as were the average parents of an Ernie, or because they were half as inventive, or because they were much, much more forgetful.

"You know where there are any surplus motorcycles?"

"Surplus?"

"Yeah."

"Motorcycles?"

"Yeah."

"Surplus motorcycles?"

"That's the concept: surplus motorcycles."

"Where the fuck did you get the idea that there are surplus motorcycles?"

"Peter."

Ernie advanced out of the perpetual gloom of the Lodkochnikov interior, astonishment and contempt struggling for dominance in his expression.

"Surplus fucking motorcycles?"

"Well—yeah."

"Hey, Ernie!" he called into the house.

"Whaddaya want, shithead?" growled the other Ernie.

"Is there such a thing as surplus motorcycles?"

"Oh, yeah. Sure."

"Where the fuck are they?"

"Somewhere over the rainbow, beyond the sea, in never-never land, on the unicorn ranch, where virgins ride them when they herd the beasts."

"That's a good one, Ernie," said the Ernie standing in front of us, shaking his head in chortling admiration. "Jesus, that's a good one."

RASKOL AND I walked down the plank that linked the front porch of their riverside house on stilts with the margin of River Sound Road. When we were well out of earshot of the two Ernies, I said, "I thought they'd know. I thought you'd know."

"Nobody can know something that can't be known," he said. "There aren't any surplus motorcycles, so there isn't any way that anybody could know where to find them." He took note of my crestfallen look and gave me a punch on the shoulder. "However," he said, "there are wrecked motorcycles, quite a few of them, and I know where they are."

"Where?"

"Pretty far. We'll have to drive. I'll pick you up tonight. Midnight."

IN DEFENSE OF THE EDITORS of *Impractical Craftsman*, I will say that I have come to think that an assumption underlay their assertion that a surplus motorcycle would be easy to obtain, a collective assumption arising from what today I can recognize as the naïveté of the incurably hopeful. I recognize it now between the lines in those old issues of *Impractical Craftsman* because I recognize it now in myself. You need a motorcycle. You want a motorcycle. You know you can't afford a new one. If only there were some surplus ones available, cheap. Surplus motorcycles? Well, gee, why not? Sure. Of course. The world must be rich in them, if there's any justice.

Chapter 25
A Sop

RASKOL did not have a New York State driver's license, nor did he have his father's license to drive the family truck. However, occasionally, at night, when the rest of his family was asleep, he would slip outside and cross the street to the weedy lot where the Lodkochnikovs parked the family truck, an old Studebaker C-Cab pickup, put his shoulder to the doorframe and roll the truck away silently, pushing it along the road until he was far enough from the house to start it without being heard, and take it for a ride. I sometimes went with him on these rides. Most of the time, we went wherever fancy took us, inventing ways to let chance determine which turn to make at the next intersection, but now and then we would get the urge to go somewhere in particular, to take a trip with a destination, and when we did, the destination was usually Montauk, the eastern tip of the south fork of Long Island. I would slip out of my house and wait for him at the corner, three houses south, distant enough so that my parents, who were sometimes wakeful, wouldn't hear the door when I climbed in and pulled it shut.

I was waiting there when Raskol pulled up in the sputtering truck.

"Something wrong with it?" I asked.

"Ahh, my father doesn't take care of this thing," he said, shaking his head. "The engine keeps quitting on me."

It did.

"See what I mean?"

"I do."

"Might be points, plugs, points *and* plugs, the coil. I don't know. You got any money?"

"Some."

"We'll stop at the all-night gas station and see what they can do."

It was the coil. There were no coils for an old C-Cab pickup in stock at the garage. The mechanic suggested that we get one at Majestic Salvage and Wrecking.

"As it happens," muttered Raskol, "that's where we're headed."

"Midnight discount?" asked the mechanic.

"Yeah," said Raskol.

We lurched off in the reluctant truck, Raskol urging it on, alternately threatening and cajoling it. When the engine quit again and we were sitting in the dark, letting it rest before he tried restarting it, he said, "I bet this sends a little shiver down your spine."

"What?"

"The way the engine quits unexpectedly."

"Not particularly—" I began.

"Doesn't it make you wonder what would happen if your engine quit while you were sky-high over St. Louis?"

It hadn't until then.

"A little, I guess," I said, shrugging in the manner of a kid with a lot of nerve. Later, when he had the truck on the road again, I began wringing my hands.

WHEN WE NEARED Majestic Salvage and Wrecking, Raskol turned the headlights off, and then the engine, and we rolled into the parking lot as quietly as one can in an old truck with weak shocks, sagging springs, and a couple of clam rakes in the bed. We settled to a stop in front of a padlocked gate in a chain-link fence. Raskol reached under the seat and pulled out a paper bag.

"Midnight snack?" I asked.

"A sop for Cerberus," he said.

"Huh?" I queried, if I remember correctly.

"There's a dog," he said. "The junkyard dog."

"Ahh," I said. "The junkyard dog. A mythic figure in American life."

"That's right, and his ancestor is Cerberus, the three-headed dog that guarded the entrance to the infernal regions."

"Oh," I said. "Of course. *The Æniad.*"

We got out of the truck, closing the doors so carefully and quietly that I would have thought no ear, not even a dog's, could have heard the sound, but no sooner had we done so than something dark, snuffling, and snarling lumbered to the fence near us, on the other side, the inside. Raskol quoted from Dryden's translation of the *Æniad,* whispering:

"'No sooner landed, in his den they found / The triple porter of the Stygian sound . . .'"

"'Grim Cerberus,'" I finished.

"I've been working on this dog for quite a while," he whispered.

"Just in case?"

"Just in case," he said.

"Amazing," I said with deep and sincere admiration.

He called into the dark, hoarsely. "Cerberus. Here, boy."

"His name is actually Cerberus?"

"Are you joking?"

"No."

"How the hell would I know if his name is Cerberus?"

"I don't know. I thought, since you called him Cerberus—"

"It's what I call him. He answers to it."

The dog, a single-headed dog, came bounding over. He didn't bark. He didn't growl. If he had not been so fearsome to look at, I would have said that he was glad to see us. Raskol reached into the bag and brought out a fistful of ground beef. He held it at arm's length like Yorick's skull and soliloquized: "'The prudent Sibyl had before prepar'd / A sop, in honey steep'd, to charm the guard. . . .' In this case, the sibyl was my sister, Ariane. What she put in this, I don't know, but she told me she uses it to get away from guys who want stuff she doesn't want to give—you know what I mean?"

"Yeah," I said, with a knowing chuckle, or, to be honest, a simulation of a knowing chuckle. Raskol tossed the meat over the fence. Cerberus watched it arc and leapt to catch it as it fell. It was my turn to quote: "'He gapes; and straight, / With hunger press'd, devours the pleasing bait. / Long draughts of sleep his monstrous limbs enslave; / He reels, and, falling, fills the spacious cave.'"

Chapter 26
An Urge

"WHEN THE DOG WAS CLEARLY UNCONSCIOUS, we clambered over the fence and inside the yard," I wrote. During the act of writing, while bringing the fence to mind and recalling our clambering over it, the thought occurred to me that today we probably wouldn't have been able to get beyond that fence. It would have concertina wire strung along the top, wire that bore, at intervals, projections in the shape of trapezoids, the inverted bases of decapitated triangles, razor-sharp, far sharper than the teeth of Cerberus, and a better deterrent to teenage midnight salvage. I got the urge—

As I age, I am continually amazed by the vastness of my ignorance. "I got the urge" is another example of it, an expression that I have taken for granted, and I see now what a limp one it is. Mr. MacPherson, wherever you are, you will, I think, be happy to know that I looked it up. The origin of *urge,* the Latin word *urgere,* "to press, force, or drive," suggests something much more active than the expression does. It suggests that there is a someone or something doing the pressing, forcing, or driving—a god, perhaps. I'll try again—

Urge, the Roman god of curiosity and shopping, powerful and compelling, beloved of Pandora, entered my bedroom through the open window and began pressing me to drive out to Long Island, beyond Babbington, to see what the junkyard might look like now. Did it still exist? Had it been replaced by a gated community of "luxury" condominiums? Something called, say, Majestic Acres? Or Mirabasura? Albertine and I could pack a lunch, drive out, find the junkyard or its replacement, and then picnic on the beach, weather permitting.

"Are you asleep?" I whispered, softly, in Al's direction.

"No. Do you want to read?"

"Actually, I was thinking about going for a drive."

"We don't have a car."

"We could borrow one."

"From whom?"

"Just kidding," I said, as if the whole thing had been the best I could manage in the way of a joke in the middle of the night.

I hadn't really been kidding, though. I think that, inspired by my memories of the midnight discount escapade, I must have been playing with the idea of finding a car that we could appropriate for a couple of hours in the middle of the night, when its owner wouldn't notice that it was gone, someone who would be as unknowingly openhanded with his car as Raskol's father had been with his truck. I astonished myself. Perhaps you think that I was astonished and a bit ashamed to find that I was even thinking of "borrowing" someone else's property. I was, a bit, but I've been living in Manhattan for a while now, and my sense of the rightness of ownership has decayed. I was more astonished to recognize that I did not possess the skills required to borrow a car without license to do so. I didn't even know how to jump the ignition. How could it be that I had gone through an entire youth and young-adulthood in the United States of America in the twentieth century without learning such a skill?

"We could rent one," I suggested.

"Or," she said sleepily, "here's an idea—you could build one—"

"Hey."

"—out of the parts of abandoned Pinch-a-Penny projects."

"Ouch."

"Not such a bad idea, really."

"Come on, Al."

"It could be a real city car."

"Is this a joke?"

"It was, but now I'm wondering."

"Wonder on."

"Room for two, and room for shopping bags—"

"Shopping bags, of course."

"—shelter from the rain and snow—"

"This is starting to sound like—"

"That little white plane you were looking at this afternoon."

"How often are you looking over my shoulder?"

"When there's a picture on your screen, it's hard to resist."

"That was the Mistral, that little plane."

"It was attractive, chic, sleek, like a shoe."

"It's French."

"Ah! I should have known."

"It is a sleek little thing."

"Very. And when I saw it, I thought at once that it would make a beautiful little city car, without the wings."

"It's really just one wing."

"It's not as sleek or chic as the rest of the plane."

"You're right."

"It's so big, and so rectangular."

"I was thinking the same thing myself."

"That it would make a good car?"

"No. That the wing looked clumsy compared to the rest of it."

"So, subtract the wing—"

"—and lop off the tail, which sticks out like an afterthought—"

"—something tagging behind—"

"—like a trailer—a dog on a leash—"

"—a clerk in a shoe store who hovers when you want to browse the stock at your leisure, raising each shoe, assessing its heft, fingering its heel—"

"Good night again, my darling."

"Good night."

I lay there for a long while, imagining a flight in the sleek Mistral, out to Long Island, for a low overflight of Majestic Salvage and Wrecking. I was pleased to see that it was still there. There was no razor wire. Two kids, the age I once was, were clambering over the fence. They froze when they heard the Mistral humming overhead and ran when I buzzed them. I don't know why I buzzed them. It was just an urge.

Chapter 27
Majestic Salvage and Wrecking

WHEN THE DOG WAS CLEARLY UNCONSCIOUS, we clambered over the fence and inside the yard. Raskol had a flashlight. He switched it on, then off again at once. "The motorcycles are over in that direction," he said, meaning the direction in which he had shone the beam.

"How do you know?" I asked, not because I doubted him but because I wondered how he knew.

"I come here during the day now and then and buy something. It gives me a chance to browse."

"Wow," I said, in deep admiration of his thoroughness and foresight and, I think I realize now, his daring and his audacity in taking such a step toward an outlaw's life.

The night was dark, but after a few minutes I could see the vague outlines of masses of things, and plenty of them, though I couldn't have said what most of them were. We had to step carefully as we made our way in the direction of the motorcycles. Everywhere in our path lay items awaiting salvage. Junk, one might say, but why demean it by calling it that? What should properly be called junk, I think, is only what is useless, nothing more than trash, but what surrounded us in such looming profusion was useful stuff. That is, it was *potentially* useful. All of it had outlived its original use, but it was waiting here in limbo for a new life, waiting to be salvaged, put to a new use, the way memories that seem to have been forgotten wait in the dark recesses of the majestic salvage and wrecking yard of the mind, patient in that limbo until they are salvaged and put to a new use.

I remember seeing in *Impractical Craftsman* an article that told how to make a power saw out of an engine block and another that featured a potter's wheel made from the guts of a washing machine. Nothing is ever completely useless: that was the *IC* creed. If you looked at things with that *IC* mind-set, there was no such thing as junk. Everything that had lost its original value, that was no longer fit for its original use, had another potential use. It was the philosophy of reincarnation applied to anything too old and worn and broken to do what it was accustomed to do, but not dead yet if someone would come along and recognize the potential within it, recognize that it was not a piece of junk but an object awaiting salvage and re-employment.

One might have been able to establish a religion on the *IC* philosophy, a religion that asserted as doctrine the continuing usefulness of everything, the Doctrine of Perpetual Utility.

Proust might have become a congregant. He wrote, in the Overture to *Swann's Way,* "I feel that there is much to be said for the Celtic belief that the souls of those whom we have lost are held captive in some . . . inanimate object, and so effectively lost to us until the day (which to many never comes) when we happen to . . . obtain possession of the object which forms their prison. Then they start and tremble, they call us by our name, and as soon as we have recognized their voice the spell is broken. We have delivered them: they have overcome death and return to share our life."

He had the *IC* spirit, Marcel. All the objects we have ever encountered in life, even simulacra of the objects we have encountered in life, have the potential of enjoying a second life. When we recall them we resurrect their original significance, and when we recount for others our experiences with them we construct a new significance for them, we revivify them. In the weltanschauung of *Impractical Craftsman* and *A la Recherche du Temps Perdu*, and *The Personal History, Adventures, Experiences & Observations of Peter Leroy,* there is no junk.

"What is all this stuff?" I asked in an awestruck gasp. It seemed to me a chaotic profusion of unidentifiable masses, a landscape made of who knew what.

"Cars over there, stacked on top of one another. Trucks there. The bodies, that is. Engines over there. Transmissions behind them. Driveshafts, axles, wheels. Appliances in that section. Stoves, refrigerators, washing machines . . ." He shrugged and did not continue. The enumeration would have been too much and, he suggested in the shrug, unnecessary, because it would have amounted to the enumeration of all the mechanical devices one might have listed as the machinery of human life in the middle of the twentieth century. He left it to me to continue the list on my own if I wished.

"It's like those maps," I said, "the ones in the atlas that show the products for every state, with little cars scattered over Detroit and South Bend and wheels of cheese all over Wisconsin." A map like that had taken shape in my mind, a map of Majestic Salvage and Wrecking that had replaced my original impression of chaos with a neat overhead view, with little wrecked cars in one region, little broken stoves in another.

"We're there," he said. He stopped. I stopped.

We were standing in an area that at first seemed not to be distinguished in any way from any of the other areas, but then, gradually, I began to be able to see that we were surrounded by lean creatures standing frozen like a herd of the metal deer that people bought to decorate their front lawns. I put my hand out and felt the rack of one, the flank of another.

"Motorcycles," I said, with the reverence of a naturalist.

"Motorcycles," Raskol said in confirmation.

We began prowling among them, running our hands over them, bending close to peer at their mechanics, giving them a shake now and then to see what was loose. As I moved among them, I began to feel like a battlefield medic, one of the skinny, ill-trained, well-meaning kids I'd seen in so many war movies at the Babbington Theater. Most of the motorcycles that I examined in the dark felt like hopeless cases, calling into question the precepts of the Doctrine of Perpetual Utility and making me feel that I should call for one of the grizzled, wise, infinitely compassionate battlefield padres I'd seen in the same war movies.

With thoughts of war and death and movies in my mind, I was hardly surprised to hear a deep and rumbling voice from somewhere in the mysterious darkness ask, "How you planning to get one of those 'cross the fence?"

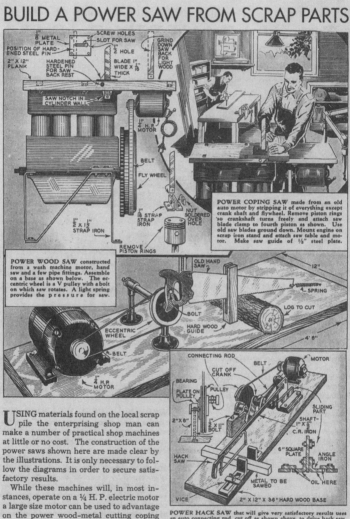

BUILD A POWER SAW FROM SCRAP PARTS

POWER COPING SAW made from an old auto motor by stripping it of everything except crank shaft and flywheel. Remove piston rings so crankshaft turns freely and attach saw blade clamp to fourth piston as shown. Use old saw blades ground down. Mount engine on scrap iron stand and attach saw table and motor. Make saw guide of ⅛" steel plate.

POWER WOOD SAW constructed from a wash machine motor, hand saw and a few pipe fittings. Assemble on a base as shown below. The eccentric wheel is a V pulley with a bolt on which saw rotates. A light spring provides the pressure for saw.

USING materials found on the local scrap pile the enterprising shop man can make a number of practical shop machines at little or no cost. The construction of the power saws shown here are made clear by the illustrations. It is only necessary to follow the diagrams in order to secure satisfactory results.

While these machines will, in most instances, operate on a ¼ H. P. electric motor a large size motor can be used to advantage on the power wood-metal cutting coping saw. The power hack saw and wood saw require only a light motor for successful operation.

POWER HACK SAW that will give very satisfactory results uses an auto connecting rod, cut off as shown above, to drive hack saw. A large wooden pulley powered by a ¼ H. P. electric motor operates connecting rod. Metal is held rigid by simple vise.

Impractical Craftsman

I remember seeing in *Impractical Craftsman* an article that told how to make a power saw out of an engine block . . .

Chapter 28
I, Sven

RASKOL AND I turned toward each other. There was a moment when each of us thought that the other had asked the question, but that error lasted only a moment. The voice still seemed to rumble in the yard, deeper and older than either of us could have managed if we had affected a tone meant to rattle the other.

My first thought was to run, but my legs would not respond to the order. Apparently they did not agree that running was the right strategy. I looked at them, astonished that they should disobey me in such a comical manner, behaving, as they were, like the legs of a frightened boy in an animated cartoon.

To my further astonishment, Raskol answered the question, while swiveling his head to try to find its source. "We're going to fly one out," he said. "Like Icarus and Dædalus."

"That stunt didn't work none too well, as I recall," said the voice. Resurrecting that voice from Majestic Salvage and Wrecking now, I hear in it something that I did not hear then. I hear in its dark depth of sound a measure of concern for our safety, a certain quality that tends toward a plea. It's not a matter of pitch or volume so much as a timbre, a tenseness in the vocal cords, perhaps. A timbre like that came into my mother's voice when she cautioned me about the dangers of snorkeling or dating. At the time, in the salvage yard, I didn't hear it. I heard only the threat of capture, interrogation, trial, sentencing, imprisonment, durance vile, and physical harm of some kind—unspecified and therefore as horrible as I

could imagine. "Icarus crashed, you know," the voice added, and if I'd
known how to hear it, I would have detected something like regret.

"We're not going to crash," said Raskol. "We've got plans. From a
magazine."

"Hmm," said the voice. "Plans. Let's see 'em."

"I don't think we've got them with us," said Raskol. "Have you got the
plans, Peter?"

My voice had allied itself with my legs in a policy of passive resis-
tance. I wanted to speak—not as much as I wanted to run, but I did want
to speak, since Raskol seemed to be having some success with speaking
as a tactic, if only a delaying tactic. I may have been inhibited by the formula I had heard so often in cop movies: "Anything you say may be taken
down and used in evidence against you."

"Peter?" Raskol prodded.

"Wahuhih," I said, though I may be misspelling that.

"You Danish?" asked the voice.

"Nuühahnah," I said, approximately.

"Norwegian?" asked the voice.

"Swedish," said Raskol.

"Don't he speak no English?"

"Ooka hap-pa nih ka heppa wah Eng-leesh, Sven?" Raskol asked me
with exaggerated enunciation.

"Heppa wah Eng-leesh," I said, and found that I had regained my
voice. "Are you going to arrest us?" I asked, with an attempt at a Swedish
accent.

The shape in the dark began to rumble good-naturedly. I wouldn't call
it laughing, but there was a jovial quality to it. "That's a good one," the
voice said. "Me on the lam, and you asking if I'm going to arrest you."

"You're on the lam?" I said, more thrilled than I can tell. This was
wonderful news. We were within the limits of the town of Babbington,
although we were outside the village of Babbington, so I was quite specifically right there in my own home town, and I was consorting with someone who was on the lam. I felt, and I was thrilled to feel, like one of the
innocent people in movies whose humdrum lives were interrupted and en-
livened by their being mistaken for crooks or murderers and driven by
mistaken identity into fleeing the cops. It made my town a much richer

place than it had been just a few minutes ago. I wondered if he was carrying a gat. "Have you got a gat?" I asked.

"A gat?"

"A rod. A heater."

"You've been watching too many American movies, Sven."

"I take it you're not employed by Majestic Salvage and Wrecking,"
said Raskol.

"Ain't employed by nobody."

"You're not the night watchman?"

"Not the chief of police, neither. Just a resident."

"A resident?"

"That's right. I live here."

"Here?" I said. "In the junkyard?"

"It may be a junkyard to you, but it's home to me."

"Of course," I said. "I'm sorry. I—"

"I got it made in the shade, Sven. Most of what I need I got right here
in the yard. Prowl around this place long enough, you find all the com-
forts of home. I got a nice little place carved out of a couple of cars at the
bottom of the heap over there. Hidden. You'd never find your way to it.
Not a chance. Got a nice sofa, coffee table, refrigerator. The only thing I
don't find here is my domestic items and consumables. Food and drink.
Soap. Linens. Sundry items of that sort. But that stuff's easy to steal outside. I make my little forays over the fence, come back with my provi-
sions. Even the dog don't bother me much. He's got so's he's used to me.
Not that we exactly get along. Don't neither of us trust the other much.
Sometimes I get the feeling that he's not going to let me back in after one
of my shopping sprees. You got him good with that meat you threw him,
though. Did you kill him?"

"No," said Raskol. "Just put him to sleep for the night."

"I'd like to have that recipe, if you don't mind."

"It's my sister's secret, but I think I can get you a little bottle of the
active ingredient."

"Much obliged. Now about that motorcycle you're after."

"I don't think any one of them is going to do the trick," said Raskol.

"They are in pretty bad shape."

"I think we need the working parts of a few of them," I said.

"Plenty of tools available, and I'm pretty handy. When we got 'em dismantled, we can just heave the pieces over the fence."

"Thanks," I said. "That's a great idea. Let's—"

"Let's negotiate a price."

"A price?"

"That's what I said."

"But they're not yours," I objected.

The big presence rumbled again. If the rumble was laughter, it was laughter that said that the issue of ownership was no laughing matter.

"How much have you got on you?" Raskol asked in a murmur.

"A couple of dollars," I said.

"Me, too."

"You think he'll go for that?"

"We can ask."

"We've got four dollars," Raskol said in the direction of the presence.

"In all the world?" the presence rumbled.

"Four dollars and the knockout drops," said Raskol.

"I thought you had to get those drops from your sister."

"I do. I'll bring them tomorrow."

"Oh. I see. You'll give me four dollars now, and we'll dismantle the motorcycles, salvage the parts you need, and toss them over the fence. Then you'll make your exit from here, go round the fence, load the parts into that truck with the bad shocks, and drive off, and tomorrow night you'll come back and bring me a little vial of those knockout drops."

"That's the plan," Raskol said hopefully.

"And it sounds like a good plan to me," said the presence, "but—"

He paused. Reflecting on the episode now, reliving it, I recognize the pause for what it was: a deliberate pause, a pause for effect, and it had its intended effect. Raskol and I stood still, waiting for what was to follow, and when, after a while, nothing did, Raskol asked what the presence intended us to ask: "'But' what?"

"You're going to have to leave the Swedish meatball as a hostage."

The word *hostage* had a powerful incantatory effect on my recalcitrant legs. On *hos* I felt energy rush through me, as if the effect of adrenaline were an electric force, and when I heard *tage* the syllable struck me like a jockey's whip. The spell of immobility was broken and I was off, as they say, like a shot.

I ran headlong through the dark, trying to pick my way among the items awaiting salvage, and doing the sort of job you would expect a frightened kid to do in the dark: banging my knees, stumbling, falling, running in blind haste and fear. Raskol was right beside me, so I felt no shame in running, and from the way his breath was coming in bursts and gasps, I felt no shame in being afraid, either. Behind us, we heard the rumbling laughter of the presence, diminishing with distance, and if we had taken a moment to consider what we heard, we would have realized that he wasn't pursuing us and we would probably have concluded that he had been amusing himself at our expense and that he had no intention of putting himself to the trouble of running after us. Instead, we just kept running, stumbling, falling, picking ourselves up, and running again, until we reached the front gate, where Cerberus lay still and sleeping, scrambled over the fence, got into the truck, and drove off, spinning the tires, spraying gravel.

Chapter 29
In Which My Conscience Makes an Appearance

ALBERTINE AND I had given ourselves a brief vacation, a getaway on the weekend of my birthday. We had taken the train to Montauk, at the tip of the south fork of the east end of Long Island, and then the ferry to East Phantom, the largest of the islands in the Phantom Archipelago that stretches from Montauk to Block Island. Autumn offered off-season rates; a night in an inn would be cheap. The sun was weak, but the day was calm. We unfolded our tricky beach chairs and installed their canvas seats. We sat, bundled, enjoying the sun, reading, like inmates at an alpine sanatorium.

In preparation for the writing of this book, I was reading the first volume of my memoirs, *Little Follies*. I hadn't read it in years.

"Is that any good?" Al asked.

"Not as bad as I feared," I said. "I made some mistakes about my schoolmates, especially the one I call Spike—and some about Raskol, too, for that matter—and I seem to have gotten confused about Porky White's age and when he went to high school. Maybe I've never really known his age. Maybe he was chasing the girls at Babbington High at an age when I, the naïve I who wrote this, didn't expect him to be pursuing high school girls, well after he and my mother graduated, even after I was born."

"I wouldn't be surprised," she said.

"Now that I think about it, that's when he was driving a school bus and working at his father's bar at night."

"As I recall, there are lots of high school girls on school buses."

"Sure. That would explain it—well enough."

"You don't sound convinced. Would you like to stop in Babbington on the way back to the city—walk around—make a few discreet inquiries—take some mental notes—get a bowl of chowder—some fried clams?"

"No," I said, "but thanks for suggesting it." Then, after a pause: "Maybe." And then, after another pause: "We'll see."

We went back to our books. After a while I put my finger in the pages of *Little Follies* to mark my place and closed my eyes. I dozed. I had a few minutes of excellent sleep, one of those catnaps that leave me refreshed in a way that an entire night's sleep never does. When I woke, I turned my head toward Albertine, smiling with the pleasure of the sleep I'd had, and found her turning her head toward me, smiling with the pleasure of her own sunny autumn doze.

"We ought to learn to live in the Spanish manner," I said. "We'd be good at it."

"Mmmm," she said, relishing the thought. "A big meal in the afternoon, then sex and a siesta—"

"—then back to work till sometime in the evening—"

"—dinner at eleven and dancing till dawn."

"What time is it now?"

She raised herself on her elbows and looked to the west, where the sun was reddening at the edge of the ocean.

"Cocktail time," she said.

AT THE BAR, with a martini in hand, she grinned at me and asked, "Were you really going to steal the parts for the aerocycle?"

"I? Steal? Parts?" I asked. "How can you think that?"

"I was taken in," she said. "Are you shocked?"

"Not shocked exactly."

"Disappointed?"

"Yes. I've certainly never thought of you as someone who thought of me as a thief."

"Sometimes I like to think of you as a lovable rogue."

"Me, too!" I said, arching an eyebrow in the continental manner. "A gentleman bandit, like John Robie?"

She narrowed her eyes and studied me. "No," she said. "I guess not."

I sighed, dismissing with a Gallic shrug another childish fantasy. "The truth is that, at the time, I accepted the idea of the midnight discount."

"Oh, Peter."

"I was a kid with a dream and no money to make it come true."

"And the midnight discount was an accepted thing among your cohort?"

"I guess it was—at least among a certain subset of my cohort."

"I think it was just a little newspeak to mask the fact of theft."

"You were never a teenage boy."

"That's one of my fondest memories of my teen years."

"Let's remind ourselves that I didn't actually steal anything."

"Only because you were run off by the Monster of Majestic Salvage and Wrecking."

"By my conscience, you mean."

"That was the monster?"

"Wasn't it?"

"I don't know. Was it?"

"Maybe," I said mysteriously, in the manner of a raffish rogue.

"Maybe?"

"I think that the truth was something like this: I may have anticipated that if we had gone ahead with the plan to steal the motorcycle parts, then, later, at some unpredictable time, perhaps while I was on the road, making my way westward, on a dark and lonely night, a large and threatening presence would appear to me and suggest that I had better own up to my crime and make some restitution . . . or else."

"I wonder if you are the last man alive with such a fearsome conscience," she said, musing.

Chapter 30
A Worthy Cause

THE NEXT MORNING Raskol and I met at Cap'n Leech's hovel before returning to Majestic Salvage and Wrecking as legitimate customers. Cap'n Leech had once owned a boatyard on the estuarial stretch of the Bolotomy River, not far upstream from the Lodkochnikov house. The boatyard now belonged to his son, Raoul, who had put his father out to pasture in a hovel built from a kit, a temporary shelter that was meant to be a storage shed, a garage for a second car, or a place within which the backyard tinkerer could work in bad weather, but never a home. Because Raoul recognized that he had not provided for his father the comfortable old age that the honored ancestor deserved, Raoul gave the Cap'n some cash now and then. It was conscience money. Raoul may have discovered that from time to time, particularly on dark and lonely nights, a large and threatening presence appeared to him and suggested that he'd better take a few bills to the old man, or else. The Cap'n had no real need for this money. When he gave the boatyard to Raoul, he hadn't expected a pension; he had expected a deep and abiding gratitude for the gift, and for the lifetime of work that had gone into building the boatyard into a business that Raoul could run and enjoy. Specifically, he had expected that he would be given some sinecure there that allowed him a place where he could sit and smoke and spit and shoot the shit with his cronies, happy in the atmosphere of motor oil and bottom paint and varnish that he had known for so long, but without the burden of work. That was what he had wanted, but that was not at all what Raoul had wanted. Raoul had feared that his father, if allowed to remain within the boatyard, would have remained the badgering presence that he had been throughout Raoul's childhood and youth, always demanding, always finding fault, always belittling, but now with the additional expectation of gratitude. So Raoul banished the Cap'n from the boatyard, on pain of anger and ridicule if he should dare to return. In his hovel, the old man smoldered with resentment. He accepted Raoul's conscience money but refused to spend it. Friends brought him what he needed, and Raskol was one of the most loyal of these. The Cap'n stuffed the cash in burlap sacks and used the sacks as seating. He had often said to Raskol, sometimes in my presence, that if Raskol ever needed money "for a worthy cause," they could always dip into his furniture.

"Good morning, Cap'n," Raskol called, standing at the closed door of the hovel.

The door swung open.

"Young Master Lodkochnikov—and young Master Leroy."

"I brought you an egg sandwich and a snapshot of my sister," said Raskol.

"I brought you a Coffee-Toffee," I said.

"What's that?" he asked.

"It's soda."

He examined the bottle as if he had never seen a bottle of Coffee-Toffee before, though that seemed unlikely to me because Coffee-Toffee was the most popular soft drink in that time and place, and there were Coffee-Toffee vending machines all over town.

"Have you no sister?" he asked.

"No, Cap'n," I said. "We've been through that before."

"Oh, yes, yes," he wheezed. "I remember now."

"You were checking on me, weren't you?"

He let slip his reedy, wheezing laugh, "hee-hee-hee," and gave me a playful whack with his cane. "I was!" he said, as if he'd done something extraordinarily clever. "You'd be amazed how many people come here and tell me lies." He drew us toward him, clutched our arms with his bony hands, and leaned inward to ensure that no eavesdropper would hear. "They all want to get the stuffing!" he said, and then released the reedy laugh again.

"That's why we're here," said Raskol.

The Cap'n's eyes popped suddenly and spectacularly, as if Raskol had wrapped him in a bear hug and squeezed. "'Et tu, Brute?'" he gasped.

"You always told me that if I needed money—"

"For a worthy cause!" he cried, swinging the cane in an arc that made us duck. "For a worthy cause! Only for a worthy cause!"

"It is for a worthy cause!" shouted Raskol.

The Cap'n had tired himself. He sank to one of the burlap sacks. He stabbed his finger in the direction of the egg sandwich, and Raskol gave it to him. I gave him the Coffee-Toffee bottle, and he opened it with the beer-can opener that he wore as an amulet on a leather thong around his neck. He refreshed himself with a couple of bites of the sandwich and a long pull at the soda.

"I wasn't expecting any worthy causes until after I was dead," he said, almost tearily. "After that," he added, swiveling his head to survey his domain and ending with his eyes fixed on Raskol's, "all this will be yours." I think my jaw dropped at that revelation; if it is true that people's jaws do drop when they hear startling revelations, then mine must certainly have dropped then; the Cap'n had no mirrors, so I couldn't check, and cannot check in recollection now, since memory refuses to supply the Cap'n with any mirrors, but I think that my jaw dropped, and I gaped. "All yours when I'm gone," he said, "but for now, I'd prefer to keep it myself. I've kind of gotten used to having it around." He squeezed the sack that he was sitting on, and it crinkled internally. "I suppose your mother is in desperate need of a costly operation?"

"No—" said Raskol.

"The bank is threatening to foreclose on the family shack?"

"No—"

"Your sister has to—ah—preserve what's left of her reputation?"

"No," said Raskol. "It's for Peter."

The Cap'n looked at me, studying me, trying to decide why I might need to dip into his furniture. After consideration, he said, "Up to your eyeballs in debt, are you?"

"No," I said, chuckling, little realizing how accurately the Cap'n had predicted the balance sheet for most of the years of my adult life.

"It's for his education," said Raskol. "He's been accepted at the prestigious Faustroll Institute in New Mexico, and he—"

"Pfweh," said the Cap'n dismissively.

"—has to build an airplane to get there."

"What?" the old man said, directing the question at me.

"I'm going to build it out of parts of surplus—I mean wrecked—motorcycles," I said. "I've got plans."

"Damn," he said, and this time he definitely did have a tear in his eye. "Damn."

"What's the matter?" I asked.

Shaking his head slowly, he said, "That is a worthy cause—damn it."

Chapter 31
El Patrón's Revenge

BECAUSE RASKOL HADN'T yet developed the skill to borrow the family truck in broad daylight, we hitchhiked to Majestic Salvage and Wrecking. While we were standing beside the road with our thumbs out and our pockets stuffed with the crumpled bills we'd extracted from Cap'n Leech's furniture, waiting for an obliging motorist to come by, I said, "Holy mackerel, Raskol, you're going to be rich!" summing up in those few words the surprise and awe that had been inspired within me by the Cap'n's revelation about his intended disposition of those comfy sacks of cash.

I recognized, even as I said it, that I also felt a bit of disappointment. There was the possibility that I wouldn't be around to see Raskol come into his inheritance. Just when I had found a way to get out of Babbington, if only for a summer, the town had begun to reveal depths hitherto unrevealed. Here was my best friend secretly tapped as the inheritor of wads of folding money, wealth beyond anything his family or mine had ever known. He was going to need a pal to help him haul the sacks away when the Cap'n kicked the bucket, and I might not be around to be that pal. I might be in distant New Mexico.

"Rich," he said. "Yeah—but not for long."

"What do you mean?" I asked.

"I know what I'm supposed to do with the money. It comes with an obligation."

This was getting better and better.

"What's the obligation?"

"I'm required to use the money to bring Raoul to his knees. Drive him out of business. Start a small boatyard of my own. Undercut him on every piece of nautical gear and every boatyard service. And when he's on the edge of bankruptcy, deep in debt and desperate for cash, buy him out for a fraction of what the place is worth, make him an offer he can't refuse, a very specific offer."

"What's that?"

"A small annuity and lifetime tenancy in the hovel he built for his father."

"Wow," I said. "You're an agent of justice—more than that—you're an avenging angel!"

"I'm no angel," he said with a practiced sneer.

"This could be a western," I said, thrilled beyond the telling. "Instead of a boatyard, Cap'n Leech—but he wouldn't be a captain, of course, not in a western—instead of a boatyard, he'd have a ranch, a huge ranch—"

A car stopped for us, and we got in.

"Where are you going, boys?" asked the driver. It was Mr. MacPherson.

"Majestic Salvage and Wrecking," I said. "Thanks for picking us up, Mr. MacPherson."

"Glad to be of service," he said. "I can drop you off on the other side of the tracks."

"That's fine," said Raskol. "Thanks."

"The Cap'n," I resumed, "or whatever you call a guy who owns a ranch—"

I paused. I expected Mr. MacPherson to supply the word.

"Hmmm," he said thoughtfully. "I don't think there is a specific word, other than *rancher,* which could loosely be applied to anyone engaged in the business of ranching, whether he was the head of the operation or not, but I suppose that you are looking for something more comparable to *captain* than to *shipping magnate,* so in this case, assuming that the ranch is in the Southwest, you might call him the *patrón,* or even El Patrón."

"Thanks. El Patrón has acres and acres, stretching across the High Plains, and he has spent the best years of his life turning his ranch into the finest spread west of the Mississippi, with the best beef cattle west of the—um—Mississippi. Years earlier he had graduated from Harvard, with a law degree, but found that the cities of the East were too confining to accommodate the breadth of his dreams and ambitions, so he came out west and settled in Dry Gulch. There he met and fell in love with a young schoolmarm, Miss Clementine, who had come west after graduating from the Baltimore Normal School, her heart afire with a mission to educate and civilize the wild offspring of the other pioneers and homesteaders, bringing with her the beginnings of the finest library west of the—ah—Monongahela. Sadly, after their storybook marriage, she died in child-birth, and the Cap'n—El Patrón—was left with nothing but the dry earth and his cattle and his infant son, Raoul. From the start, Raoul was a prob-lem child. He was stubborn and rebellious and—uhh—pusillanimous."

"Bellicose," said the driver, since he was, after all, Mr. MacPherson.

"Oh, yeah," I said. "Not pusillanimous. Bellicose. He was bellicose, and El Patrón had to rescue him from one scrape after another. Finally, the boy came of age. The old Patrón took him to the porch of the grand house that had grown from the humble shack that he had originally built, put his hand on his boy's shoulder and said, 'Raoul, today you have be-come a man, and today you have become a landowner.' Looking out over the vast expanse of Rancho Grande, he said, 'All this is yours, my boy.' He unfurled a deed, a simple document but handsomely engraved and properly signed and sealed, and handed it to his troublesome son. It was a touching ceremony that El Patrón had devised during the long nights when he rode his favorite horse, Thunderclap, through the darkness and into the dawn trying to rid himself of the anger he felt toward his way-ward boy and to escape the sorrow he felt over the loss of his darling Clementine, talking to her in the dark as he rode, seeking the advice that would help him tame the wild child. 'Thanks, Dad,' sneered Raoul, and within days he had had his father's personal belongings moved from the ranch house to a tent on the driest and loneliest corner of the domain, where he left the old man to desiccation and despair. Meanwhile, Raoul, as good a rancher as his father and far sharper in his business dealings, grew ever richer at the expense of the other inhabitants of Dry Gulch. He controlled the bank, and he had the mayor and sheriff in his pocket. He bought up mortgages and foreclosed when it suited him to do so, ravish-ing the virgin daughters of his debtors whenever he got the chance. The whole town lived in fear of him, and it seemed that nothing could be done to rid them of this tyrannical cattle baron until one night, when thunder rocked the plains and lightning lit the sky with angry bolts, a stranger rode into town on a black stallion, seeking shelter from the storm. He found it in the miserable tent where the aged Patrón dwelled, and in the dark, over coffee stretched to tastelessness with chicory, he listened to the old man's tale of woe and filial disrespect. 'The deed I gave him contains a reversion clause,' he told the stranger. 'I put it in there to try to cure him of his pusill—his bellicosity. It states that if Raoul is killed in a gunfight, a showdown, everything reverts to me.' The stranger nodded silently at this, put one strong gloved hand on El Patrón's shoulder, and said—"

"I'm turning here." Mr. MacPherson pulled to the side of the road.

"Thanks for the ride," I said as Raskol and I got out.

"My car's an old and crotchety beast," he said, "certainly no Thunderclap, but then, 'the biggest horse is no aye the best traiveller.'"

Raskol and I walked the rest of the way to the salvage yard, where we bought everything we thought I was going to need. The owner's brother-in-law gave us a ride home, and he heard the story of the epic Gunfight at the Rancho Grande Corral, the reversion of the ranch, and El Patrón's happy sunset years, spent largely on the expansive porch of the ranch house, in the company of his aged cronies, shooting the shit.

Chapter 32
The Best in Town!

ALBERTINE AND I did stop in Babbington on our way back to the city. We left the train station, a few blocks north of Main Street, and walked southward, along Upper Bolotomy Road, to Main, and then eastward to River Sound Road, where we turned to the south again and followed the estuarial stretch of the Bolotomy River to Leech's Boatyard. The boatyard was still called Leech's, though discreet lettering below the name read R. LODKOCHNIKOV, PROP.

"Do you want to stop in?" she asked.

"I'm not sure," I said, and I meant it.

I wasn't sure that I wanted to spend the time. Mr. MacPherson would have recognized the full implication of the phrase *spend the time*. "Ken when to spend an when to spare," he might have warned me. There is in the notion of spending time the strong suggestion that time, one's time on earth, is like money, and that one can overspend, run out, be called to account, bankrupt oneself, before one's time ought otherwise to have been up. I had little money, and I was beginning to feel that I had as little time. Having little money, I had the feeling that I should always be at work, turning time into money as well as I could, doing whatever work I could find to try to keep the household afloat. The full version of the Scottish saying that Mr. MacPherson might have quoted to me is "Ken when to spend an when to spare, and ye needna be busy." Ahhh, yes, but if in the early days of your life, when time seemed cheap and plentiful, you did not ken when to spend and when to spare, then in the later years you must needs be busy all the time.

"You're still on vacation," Albertine reminded me.

I checked my watch. Yes, I was still on vacation, but my vacation time was running out. I knew that Raskol would probably be there, at the boatyard, busy, but not so busy that he couldn't spare some time for his old friend, and I would have been glad to see him, but I decided that the time I might have spent shooting the shit with him at the boatyard would be better spent on something else. If I had had more time . . . but I didn't. One has to budget one's time when the days dwindle down to a precious few. (Sorry, Raskol.)

We passed the boatyard and continued to the street where my paternal grandparents had lived, turned onto it, and walked past the house as inconspicuously as we could while examining it, sidelong, for alterations. Only from certain angles was it recognizable as the house I had known as a child. Seen from directly across the street, it was greatly altered, or seemed greatly altered, though the actual changes were neither so many nor so extensive that I couldn't have reversed them if I had had the money to buy the place and have the work done, or if I had had the money to buy the place and the time to do the work myself. I felt a great weight of remorse and guilt for my never having prospered sufficiently to have had the money to buy the house and preserve it. It should have been then, that afternoon, just as it had been when I was a boy and sat with my grandparents on the porch on summer evenings.

"If I had ever made any real money, buckets of it," I said to Al, "we could have bought this house, and all the others—all the ones that you and I ever lived in—and preserved them as they were."

"In our permanent design collection," she said.

"Over the course of a year, we could make a progress from house to house—"

"That would have been folly," she said consolingly, squeezing my hand, "no matter how much money we had."

We had passed the house, so we thought that we could safely stop and turn and stare.

The current owners had enclosed the front porch (or perhaps the owners before them had done it; the house had passed through several hands since my grandparents had died). They had done it in a clumsy way that made the entire front of the house look like an awkward addition. They had also painted it.

"What color is that?" I asked in a whisper, as if we might have been overheard.

"I guess I'd call it saffron," said Al.

"I'd call it aggressive," I said, "an assault on the past, battery of the memory."

I think that whoever had decided on this bellicose use of color had meant to make the house appear larger thereby, but to my eyes the brightness had diminished it. Formerly, it had been a dark gray, and the quiet dignity of the color had made the small house seem much more solid and staunch, made it more of a presence, than this saffron did.

We went on our way, made the next right, and headed back up to Main Street, where we hoped to find a place where I might get some clams, freshly dug from Bolotomy Bay, full-bellied, fried golden and crunchy. As we walked along, we noticed a number of small signs in wire frames stuck into the front lawns of the houses we passed. Some pleaded with the passersby to support the Andy Whitley Airport, others advanced the project of a new waterfront park, and some screamed NO CONDOS!

"What do you suppose that's about?" I asked.

"The airport, a park, and condominiums, I'd say," she said. "Chips in play in the game of defining Babbington's future."

"Mmm," I said, in the manner of one aloof from the fray of small-town politics.

We had reached Main Street. Only five years had passed since Albertine and I had left Babbington, but the mix of businesses along the town's throbbing commercial thoroughfare had changed considerably in that time. The diner had become a sushi bar. Many of the shops that had been idiosyncratic and local were now standardized outposts of national retailers. There seemed to be twice as many banks as there had been and three times as many insurance companies. There were five nail salons where formerly there had been none. The post office had become a restaurant called Not the Post Office Anymore.

"Clever," said Albertine, and I think she meant it.

We entered and were greeted by a smiling host.

"Do you have fried clams?" I asked peremptorily, even a bit contentiously, prepared to turn on my heels if told that they did not.

"The best in town!" declared the host with trained confidence. "Two for lunch?"

"Umm—" I said, looking around, trying to decide what I thought of the place.

"Yes," said Albertine, and she tugged me along as the host ushered us to a table.

"Stuart will be your waiter, and he'll be right with you," the host claimed. He put menus in front of us and smiled his way off in the direction of his post at the door. Stuart arrived almost at once.

"How are you folks doing today?" he asked in a breezy tone.

"We have fallen under a dark cloud of nostalgia and regret," I said.

"I hate it when that happens," he said, pouting in sympathy. "How about a little drinky?"

As we walked along, we noticed a number of small signs . . .

"Anderson's Amber," I said. "Two pints."

"And do you know what you'd like to eat?"

"The grilled chicken sandwich," said Albertine, making an assumption, since she had not looked at the menu.

"Best in town," Stuart assured her. "Comes with Whirly-Curly Fries and a side of Super Slaw. Okay?"

"Fine."

"And for you?"

"Fried clams," I said.

"You also get Whirly-Curly Fries and a side of Super Slaw with that," he said, without assuring me that the clams were the best in town. "Okay?"

"Okay."

"Okey-dokey," he said. He swung a tiny mouthpiece into position, said, "Number nine," listened for a second, and then said, "GC platter, FC platter," and he turned to go, but Albertine caught his sleeve.

"Stuart," she said in her most confidential tone, "what can you tell us about the airport-park-condo dispute raging in town?" I think she must have given him the impression that she and I were the vanguard of a television news team and that he had a good shot at an appearance on the six o'clock report, because he leaned toward the table and spilled his guts, figuratively speaking.

"Basically, it's all about the airport and its fate," he confided. "There are three camps. One wants to keep the airport forever and even expand it some. Naturally, the people who have planes are in that group. Another group calls the airport a playground for the rich and wants to bulldoze the whole thing and make a big park out of it. The *Babbington Reporter*— that's the local paper—is behind that. And then a third group supposedly wants the airport land to build a huge development of luxury condominiums. I don't know who's behind that."

"Where do you stand, Stuart?" Albertine asked.

"Off the record," he said with a wink, "I think the condominium plan is a fake, just a scare tactic. I mean, who in his right mind would buy a luxury condominium in Babbington? And as far as a park goes, haven't we got enough parks? Who uses them anyway? Just a lot of stinking bums—excuse me—stinking homeless people. I say keep the airport. It's been a part of this town as long as anybody can remember—and it's historic. I mean, you may not know it, but this is the Birthplace of Teenage Aviation!" A soft beeping sound began to emanate from Stuart. He swung the mouthpiece into position again, said, "Number nine," listened for a second, and then said, "Roger, sir, I copy." To us, he said, in the same confidential tone he had used for the straight poop on the airport dispute, "Your orders are up."

He was gone. He was back. Brisk service was a feature of Not the Post Office Anymore. He put two pints of Anderson's and two large platters of food in front of us.

"What are these?" I asked, regarding the pale beige battered strips on my plate.

"Fried clams!" he said, as if I were an idiot. "Fresh from Ipswich, Massachusetts!"

Chapter 32
I Play the Losing Game of Translation

THE TITLE PAGE of the book that Mr. MacPherson had given me said:

Alfred Jarry

Gestes & Opinions
du
Docteur Faustroll
pataphysicien

roman néo-scientifique

I began my translation there. I hesitated at *gestes* and spent some time vacillating between translating it as *jests* or *jokes*. The obvious choice seemed to be *jests,* but it sounded antiquated, even quaint, while *jokes* sounded too casual, too—well—jokey. I was about to settle for *jests* when I recalled Mr. MacPherson's caution against the treachery of *faux-amis,* those pairs of French and English words that resembled each other enough for the student to think that they must be the same, or nearly so, when they were actually so different as to be barely on speaking terms. I turned to my French-English dictionary. It told me that a *geste* was a gesture, a motion or movement, an action, or a wave of the hand. Hmmm. The gestures and opinions of Doctor Faustroll? Not likely. The actions, then. No. Acts. No. Too inactive somehow. Deeds? Accomplishments? Adventures? Adventures. If it were *my* book, I would certainly prefer *ad-*

ventures to *acts* or *actions* or even *accomplishments*. Thus:

Alfred Jarry

Adventures & Opinions
of
Doctor Faustroll
Pataphysician

A Neo-Scientific Novel

I could have stopped there and counted it as a page done, but, flushed with success, I decided to push on. "Livre Premier: Procèdure" I translated as "Book One: Procedure," and the first part of that book I translated as follows:

I
COMMANDMENT
IN ACCORDANCE WITH ARTICLE 819

IN THE YEAR eighteen hundred ninety-eight, on the eighth of February, in accordance with article 819 of the Code of Civil Procedure and at the request of Mr. and Mrs. Bonhomme (Jacques), owners of a house situated in Paris, at 100$^{1/2}$ Richer Street, for which residence, abode, house, or premises I am the elected member in my residence, dwelling, or abode and also in the registry office of the Qth or 15th District, I, the undersigned, René-Isidore Panmuphle, bailiff within the civil tribunal of the first instance of the district of the Seine, situated in Paris, residing there, at 37 Pavée Street, have made Commandment in accord with the Law and Justice, to Mr. Faustroll, doctor, tenant or lodger in various premises annexed to the aforementioned house situated in Paris at 100$^{1/2}$ Richer Street, where having gone to the aforementioned house, upon which was found equally indicated the number 100, and after having rung the bell, knocked, and called the above-named on different repeated occasions, no one having come to open the door for us, the nearest neighbors declared to us that it was indeed the residence or domicile of the said Mr. Faustroll, but that they were not willing to accept the copy and whereas I did not find at the aforesaid premises either parents or servants, and none of the neighbors was willing to assume the duty of being presented with the copy upon signing my original, I returned immediately to the registry office of the Qth or 15th District, whereupon I returned to the Mayor, speaking with him personally, who gave me his initials or signature on my original: within twenty-four hours as a total extension of time, to pay to the plaintiff in my hands for which will be tendered to him good and valuable receipt the sum of three hundred seventy-two thousand francs and 27 centimes, for eleven terms of rent on the above-named premises, due the following January first, without prejudice of those falling due and all other rights, actions, interests, fresh or newly put into execution, declaring to him that failing to satisfy under the present Commandment in the said extension of time, there will be or he will be compelled by all the ways or means of right or law, and notably by the seizure as security or in payment of furnishings, furniture, and personal belongings, furnishing or filling the rented premises. And I have at the domicile or residence as I have said below left the present copy. Cost: eleven francs 30 centimes, which includes 1/2 sheet with a special stamp at 0 francs 60 centimes.

PANMUPHLE

Monsieur le Docteur Faustroll in the registry of the Qth or 15th District, Paris.

MY TRANSLATION wasn't all that it might have been. I recognized that. It ran like an engine with dirty plugs, sputtering and stuttering until at last it coughed and died. An engine like that was not fit to pull a plane from Babbington to New Mexico, and a translation like that wasn't going to be enough to endear a matriculating youngster to the faculty of the Faustroll Institute, if such an organization actually existed or could be found, nor was it likely to gain him entry into the prestigious ranks of Advanced French and the racy stuff its privileged students were rumored to read. I decided to sleep on it, give myself a day or so away from it, and then dismantle it and tune it up.

Chapter 33
Elements of Aeronautics

THE ADVENTURES & OPINIONS OF DOCTOR FAUSTROLL was not the only text that I studied in preparation for my journey to New Mexico and matriculation at the Faustroll Institute. I had on my own bookshelf, in my bedroom, a text that not only played a part in inspiring me to fly but taught me nearly everything I knew of the art. Years earlier, Dudley Beaker, who lived in a stucco residence or domicile on No Bridge Road beside the stucco dwelling or abode wherein resided my maternal grandparents, Herb and Lorna Piper, had given me a copy of *Elements of Aeronautics* by Francis Pope, B.A., First Lieutenant, United States Army Air Corps Reserve, and Captain (First Pilot) with Transcontinental and Western Air, Inc., and Arthur S. Otis, Ph.D., Private Pilot, Fellow of the American Association for the Advancement of Science and Technical Member of the Institute of the Aeronautical Sciences.

"Study it, Peter," he said. "Study it carefully. I think that the time is coming when air travel will become commonplace, and there will be opportunities for the young man with a prepared mind. I must confess my fear that much of the glamour of the experience of air travel will doubtless be lost when it is available to the great unwashed, but I also realize that its vulgarization will bring opportunities. If you are going to be prepared to seize those opportunities, you ought to have some idea why an airplane is capable of flight."

"And how," I said.

"What?"

"How."

"What?" he asked again, with evident irritation.

"How," I said. "I ought to know *how* it is capable of flight, too. How it flies. How it works. What makes it able to fly."

"Yes," he conceded, "I suppose you should."

Elements of Aeronautics and I were nearly the same age; the book had been published just three years before I was born. This fact struck me when I opened it and began reading it, at the very beginning, in the way that had already become my habit and has never left me. I begin with all the "front matter" that most people skip, so I've been told, often by the very people who do the skipping. There, on the copyright page, was the copyright date, and it put me in mind of my birth date, and the two made me realize in a boy's way that a book cannot do what a boy can: grow and change. In books, as Mrs. Fendreffer so often said, we can find the wisdom of the past, but she did not say that yesterday's wisdom is very often today's nonsense and that books as often turn the foolishness of the past—our myths and bigotries and superstitions—into holy writ, immutable in a changing world.

In a sense, *Elements of Aeronautics* was out-of-date, and my first glance through it showed me that the drawings were done in a style that was almost quaint, not at all the style that a contemporary publication, a new book, would have used. The article about the aerocycle from *Impractical Craftsman* was even older. It had appeared ten years before *Elements of Aeronautics* had, thirteen years before I had. In a way, I felt like the youngest of three brothers. The oldest of us was twenty-eight, a man, seriously pursuing a career in a local bank now and thinking of marriage. His early dreams of teenage aviation, inspired by that issue of *Impractical Craftsman* when it was new and didn't smell at all of mold, had never been anything more than daydreams, daydreams that he never entertained any longer, not even when a little plane came buzzing slowly overhead in the clear sky of a summer day. The middle brother was eighteen, out of school, working the bay. He had no plans for the future at all; he just worked the bay from day to day and chased the girls at night. Life was easy and simple. Why should he complicate it by attempting to learn to fly? The idea had once inspired him, made his heart seem to lift and soar, when he watched small planes taking off from the runway at the Babbington Municipal Airport, but when he had bought and tried to study *Ele-*

ments of Aeronautics, he had stumbled when he had reached Part II: Aerodynamics, and he had put the book aside, never to be taken up again. I was the little brother, only fifteen, fascinated by my older brothers and all the things that had once fascinated them, and eager to make a place for myself, a name for myself, in the trio. So I took up the daydream of the aerocycle and the old issue of *Impractical Craftsman* and the abandoned copy of *Elements of Aeronautics,* and claimed them as my own. The essential principles of aeronautics had not changed in the eighteen years since the book had been published, and motorcycles hadn't changed much since the article had been published, so their age was not a disqualification; rather, it became a recommendation, like the additional years of experience that lend weight to the pronouncements of older brothers. But, as I said above, the ossified wisdom of an earlier time, codified as writ, can bring trouble to the modern age, to modern youth.

The frontispiece to *Elements of Aeronautics* made me feel important. I memorized it. Phrases from it began to appear in my everyday conversation.

If taking my place in a nation on wings, as the frontispiece assured me I would do, made me feel important, the book's explanation of yaw, "sometimes spoken of technically as rotation about the normal axis," pitch, "sometimes spoken of technically as rotation about the lateral axis," and roll, "technically spoken of as rotation about the longitudinal axis," made me feel queasy. For each of them, I imagined myself astride the aerocycle, executing a maneuver that took each type of rotation to its exaggerated maximum: a circle, a loop, and a spin. Mentally reeling, I set the book aside. However, I knew that, unlike my imaginary older brothers, I would take it up again. I just needed enough time away from it to recover my equilibrium. Inevitably, I suppose, despite the dizziness they induced, the terms began to work their way into my vocabulary. When I rode my bicycle, I would yaw left or right instead of turning, pitch up or down a hill or bump, and now and then roll a bit from the vertical, sometimes spoken of technically as going off-kilter.

TO YOU WHO
STUDY THIS BOOK

THERE are probably several reasons why you have elected to study this book on aeronautics. Certainly you realize that there is now a job ahead for us Americans — an exacting job that calls not only for keen minds and physical fitness, but also for special kinds of training such as this book affords. Those who learn the science and art of flying, as you now propose to do, have unique opportunity to serve our country in this War of Survival that has been forced upon us. In an immediately practical way you are taking up the challenge to freedom. And when our final victory has been won, you will be ready to take your place in an America that has become a nation on wings, honored and respected by all peoples living under a democratic peace.

World Book Company, Publishers

Keep 'em Flying

BUY WAR BONDS

The frontispiece to *Elements of Aeronautics* made me feel important.

Chapter 34
Albertine Takes a Tumble

"THE CONFINES OF THE AVERAGE GARAGE," I said to Albertine.

"Ahhh, darling," she said with a sigh, "you know how I love that sweet talk."

"The confines of the average garage," I repeated seductively.

"Mmm," she moaned with pleasure.

"Those confines come up again and again in the descriptions of these build-it-yourself planes."

"All the romance has gone from garages, I see," she said, pouting.

"The people selling the kits or plans are always reassuring the prospective builder that the plane can be built 'within the confines of the average garage.'"

"And you suspect them of stretching the truth? Or shrinking the truth?"

"It's not that. It's the word that surprises me."

"*Garage*?"

"No. *Confines*."

"I prefer *garage*. If you say it right, it sounds like a term of endearment. 'Oh, how I lahhhve you, my leettle garrr-azzzh.'"

We were having this conversation on the roadway that winds through Central Park, on a Sunday afternoon. The road is closed on weekends to vehicular traffic but available to runners, walkers, skaters, dogboarders, and bicycle riders. We were on our bicycles. It was a fine day in late fall, the air cool, the sun low but warming, our spirits light.

"It surprises me that they don't just say, 'You can build it in a garage.'"

"Well, Peter, I think they want to make the point that you can build it in the space that would be available in your garage if you have a garage, but that you don't actually have to have a garage."

"Yes, but—"

"Not everyone has a garage. We don't."

"We have no car."

"Exactly. Therefore, no need for a garage. So the people selling the kits or plans may be trying to reassure the prospective builder that a garage is not actually required, just the space that your garage would contain if you had one."

"The space contained by the average garage would easily fit within the confines of our apartment," I pointed out.

She turned to deliver a rejoinder, and I saw the accident occur, the absurd events preceding it, the awful instant of coincidence, and the consequence.

To Albertine's right, a woman was dogboarding, and to her left, another woman was dogboarding. In the space of the five years that Albertine and I had been living in Manhattan, the sport of dogboarding had come from nowhere to attain a status of considerable popularity. I have heard people attempt to explain its sudden rise with the theory that it suited the predilections of many because it was an outdoor activity in which the dog did the work rather than the master, that it required gear expensive enough to give it consumer snob appeal (particularly if you counted the dog), and that it offered a physical and sensual experience that other urban sports did not, combining as it did elements of wake riding, skateboarding, and snowboarding. In addition, though, I think we should not discount the powerful appeal of its giving residents of the Upper East Side something they seem to have craved for a long time: a *reason* for housing a large dog in the confines of a small apartment.

The dogboarder's dog is outfitted with a harness similar in cut to the coats that pampered pets wear in cold weather. It fits over the dog's chest and around its forelegs and back, with reins extending rearward from the sides. Behind the dog, the boarder stands on a platform that resembles a skateboard, with the difference that instead of skate wheels the dogboard has two large wheels, miniatures of the high-tech wheels with composite rims that are used in bicycle racing, one fore and one aft, of a diameter great enough that they rise above the surface of the board, set within slots in the board and turning on axles that run through mounts below it.

I remember wondering, when I glanced at the enormous and powerful dog pulling the woman on Albertine's right, whether it had been bred expressly for dogboarding. The dog pulling the woman on Albertine's left was smaller, but not by much, and it was especially keen. It strained in its harness in a way that the larger dog did not, lunging forward whenever the other moved a bit ahead. I wondered, and I intended to discuss this with Albertine later, after they had passed by, whether the women were longtime rivals, competitors in business and within their social set and now in the dogboarding arena of Central Park. In the manner of super-heroes, both were dressed in sleek, formfitting, iridescent outfits that advertised their fitness and firmness and enhanced the resplendence of their bodies in action. They were running a playful game, crisscrossing, playing their dogs as charioteers would their steeds, tugging lightly at their harnesses to yaw the dogs this way and that. Though neither allowed the other to remain ahead, the race they were running was not a race for position but for prominence in the eye of the beholder, status as the most adept and alluring dogboarder in the city. Their rivalry had infected their dogs; they snarled at each other across the couple of feet that separated them. Later, I told myself that I should have realized that the women and their dogs posed a threat to Albertine, but they were so fluent in their movements, the dogs so good at what they were doing and the women apparently so fully in control of their dogs, that they seemed to be harmless, until the moment when Albertine turned her head, just for an instant, to reply to me, and in that moment the smaller of the dogs did something to offend the larger. What? Nothing that I can see in my mind's eye when I recall the moment. It may have been a look; it may have been something in his tone of voice, a vulgarity in his snarl; it may have been some grosser violation of the code of dogs; it may only have been that he strayed a bit from what the larger dog perceived as the proper confines of his lane. Whatever it was, it made the dog on the right respond suddenly and violently. He lunged at the dog on the left, to nip at his foreleg, I think, as a warning against persisting in that offensive behavior.

"Al!" I cried.

I saw the look on her face, saw that she was reading the look on my face. She saw the alarm there, and it made her swing around to face forward again. The dogboarding woman on the right tugged hard on the reins, but the dog was determined and resisted her. She yawed involuntarily, she fought to recover, she rolled, and her board shot from under her directly into Albertine's path. Al saw it. In an instant of peripheral awareness she turned to the left to try to avoid it, but she was on top of it. Her front wheel struck the board, and Albertine pitched forward, up and over her handlebars and onto the pavement.

I was off my bike in a moment and at her side.

"Oh, my darling, my darling," I said, kneeling beside her, kissing her, "my leettle garajzh."

She didn't seem to be in pain. She didn't seem to be hurt, only surprised, but, "Something is wrong," she said. "Something is wrong."

Chapter 35
From the Symphysis Pubis to the Crest of Ilium

SHE LAY ON A GURNEY in the hallway of the emergency room at Carl Schurz Hospital, just down the street from our apartment, just half a block from home. Hours had passed since the accident. She was in shock, I suppose, still not quite believing that this had happened to her. In the park, when she had come to rest on the pavement, she had worn that look of surprise, but now there was added to it a grimace, and I could see that she was suffering. She had cried out when the emergency medical technicians had lifted her onto the stretcher to load her into the ambulance. Here in the hospital she had been given morphine for the pain, but she could feel it through the morphine.

"Was my skirt up around my waist?" she asked.

"You're wearing shorts," I said.

"I am?"

"You are." I brought her hand to my lips. I had a flash of a memory, one of my earliest. In the memory, I was standing on my maternal grandparents' front lawn, with a kitten in either hand, looking across the lawn to where my grandparents, my parents, Dudley Beaker, and Eliza Foote were gathered for drinks in the summer dusk. Something had happened to disturb my mother, to upset her. I didn't know what it was, and wouldn't have understood it if I had, but I saw that something had upset her, disturbed her equilibrium. When I looked in the direction of the adults, I saw my mother in the act of falling from her lawn chair, and she wore the expression of surprise that I had seen on Albertine. At the time, I thought that my mother was playing, partly because of that expression of surprise. I saw, and understood in my infantile way, that she was exhilarated by crossing the line of equilibrium into a more excited state, and I laughed then, but in the hospital, with Albertine hurting so and worried that the world had seen her underwear, I saw in the mind's eye of memory that my mother had also been shocked at the moment of her tumble, astonished that this should be happening to her, and deeply embarrassed.

"Was I wearing shorts the whole time?"

"Yes, my darling."

"How prudent of me."

"Your dignity was preserved throughout."

"I doubt that," she said. She sighed. "What happened?"

"That woman's dogboard shot in front of you, and you hit it."

"Yes," she said distantly, apparently struggling to regain the memory.

"You had turned backward to say something to me, but I saw what was happening and when I called to you, you turned around, turned forward I mean, and you saw what was about to happen, so you yawed to the left, trying to avoid it. You didn't have time to turn much, not enough to avoid the board, but you did turn enough to avoid going straight over the handlebars and landing on your head."

"Did I execute a full forward somersault?"

"Head over teakettle."

"I think it's cracked."

"Head? Or teakettle?"

"Head, maybe. Teakettle, definitely."

In another couple of hours, after she had been investigated by X-ray and magnetic resonance imaging, we knew that she was right. Her pelvis had been fractured "in three places," according to the surgeon on duty in the emergency room, who later charged an inflated fee but was, in his reading of the film as well as his estimate of what his time was worth, wrong. Her pelvis had actually been fractured along a nearly continuous line from the symphysis pubis to the crest of ilium, making the integrity of the pelvis itself—so essential to supporting the body in its upright human stance and allowing it pedal mobility—tenuous, liable to a painful and perhaps irreparable shift along the fracture if she were to put her weight on her right leg, but we didn't know that until later.

"What did I say?" she asked.

"Say?" I stroked her hand. She was lying on her back. She had been told not to move.

"You told me that I turned around to say something to you. What was it?"

"I don't know. You never got to say it. Do you remember what you were going to say?"

"No. I don't remember," she said. "Something clever, I think. We would have laughed."

SOMETIME AFTER FOUR in the morning, I came out of the hospital entrance and turned toward home. I doubted that I would be able to sleep if I went home, and it was too early to call Albertine's mother and the boys to tell them what had happened, so when I reached the corner, I turned toward Carl Schurz Park instead. I couldn't stop my mind from replaying the memory of Albertine in the air, flying forward over her handlebars, yawing, pitching, and rolling in her flight, until she landed— crashed, that is—on the unyielding pavement, and then the still way she had lain there, with her legs straight out and that awful look of surprise on her face, and with it, almost superimposed on it, ran the memory of my mother, falling from her lawn chair. For both of them I felt a deep sympathy and, surprising to me, a deeper sadness for the loss of dignity that they had suffered, and I felt, as intensely as if I had fallen myself, how hard it is to hold on to dignity, to attain some scrap of dignity and then hold on to it, and I resented the way that accidents had snatched their dignity from them. I stood at the railing, looking down at the dark water of the East River, feeling useless. I couldn't mitigate Albertine's pain, couldn't alleviate it in any way, and I couldn't imagine how I could restore her dignity. While I stood there, feeling the hollow emptiness of uselessness, I began to feel something else overcome me, a familiar feeling, the overwhelming feeling of being full of my love for her. There were times, and this was one, when the experience of that love was so great that it overpowered all other emotions, rendered me incapable of feeling anything else. This state of being full of love for her was buoying, uplifting, elating, and liberating, and it lifted me, made me feel that if I chose to, I could arise and fly across the river, to Queens.

Chapter 36
Please, Sir, I Yearn to Learn

"FIRST OF ALL," said Rudolph Derringer, Certified Flying Instructor, "I want you to banish from your mind the notion that flying is dangerous." He paused and scanned the room, turning a stern and serious mien on each of his eager students. He wore a leather flying jacket with a silk scarf thrown around his neck, apparently carelessly, and a leather flying helmet with goggles pushed up on his head. "Flying is not dangerous," he said, shaking his head. He stopped. He paused. He raised a finger. And, as if the distinction had just occurred to him, he added, "*Crashing* is dangerous."

After a moment of uncertainty, we allowed ourselves a little nervous laughter. Outside, a storm was blowing through Babbington. (Was it part of the aftermath of Hurricane Felicity? I'm not sure.) Eight of us—seven men and a boy—were sitting on folding chairs in a hangar at the Babbington Municipal Airport, which was still known simply as that, since the supporters of former mayor Andy Whitley had not yet launched their campaign to have it renamed for him. Wind drove the rain against the corrugated metal siding, and we shivered in our seats.

"That's one of the maxims of the aviator," Derringer said, chuckling now. "Flying isn't dangerous; crashing is dangerous." We all chuckled along with him, dutifully, but a joke is never funny the second time around.

"You get what you pay for," muttered the man sitting beside me, dealing me an elbow in the ribs to catch my attention and pointing to the ad in the *Babbington Reporter* that had lured us to the airport.

Learn to Fly!
Your First Lesson Costs You NOTHING!
What Have You Got to Lose?
Rudolph Derringer, Certified Flying Instructor

"You get what you pay for," muttered the man sitting beside me . . .

He let his finger rest beneath the word *nothing,* and he gave me another poke in the ribs to make certain that I hadn't missed the point.

Derringer held up a battered copy of *Elements of Aeronautics.* Momentarily overcome by the desire to stand out in the crowd, court the instructor, get a head start on the competition for teacher's pet, and show that I was not only eager but prepared, I came close to announcing that I owned a copy, but, fortunately for my dignity, Derringer spoke before I had a chance to speak myself.

"You can't learn to fly from a book," he said with a sneer. He turned the cover of the book toward him and read the title as if it were an obscenity. "I sure as hell didn't learn to fly from a book. I learned to fly by the seat of my pants—and that's how I'm going to teach you to fly. You've got to *feel* the plane under you, the way you feel a horse under you when you're in the saddle. Anybody here ride?"

None of us did, and our headshakings and murmured disavowals seemed to disappoint Derringer so deeply that I thought for a moment of offering my years of bicycle riding as an approximation. Again, Derringer saved me from the guffaws of my fellows by speaking first.

"Well," he said, with evident pity, "it's a shame. If you rode, you'd know what I mean about the seat of your pants. Flying that way—it's something you feel." He stared off into the distance, upward, as if he were looking beyond the ceiling, beyond the storm and the clouds, to the limitless open space above us, his proper realm. "You become one with the plane," he said rapturously, "one airborne entity, a mythical being, a flying man, the way a rider comes to feel that he and the horse beneath him have become one, have become a mythical creature, a centaur. The seat-of-the-pants rider doesn't put his horse into a gallop; *he* gallops. And when you fly by the seat of your pants, you don't bank the plane, *you* bank. You don't roll the plane or loop the plane, *you* roll, *you* loop. Ultimately, you don't fly the plane—*you* fly."

"Ultimately, you don't crash the plane," muttered the disenchanted guy beside me. "*You* crash."

After a moment of stillness to allow the last note of his lyrical introduction to resonate, Derringer began to outline the lessons in the course that he offered, and we began to understand that the lyrical introduction was all that we were going to get for free. His presentation was on the order of what today would be called an infomercial, short on information and long on purchase opportunity. I learned, when Derringer got to the point of closing, that the cost of the course was beyond my boyish means. It may have been beyond the means of the men seated with me as well, because none of them wrote checks when they were invited to. Instead, they filed into the wet night, heads down, disappointed. I followed, adopting much the same attitude.

"It's simply amazing," said the guy who had sat beside me. "In less than a minute, Rudolph Derringer, CFI, managed to become repetitious and boring."

"Yeah," growled another guy. He took a drag on a cigarette that he held in his cupped hand to protect it from the rain. "He started out great, too. Full of promise."

"Right," said another. "When we were filing into the hangar and taking our seats, and I saw him standing there, he seemed like a dashing adventurer, a living advertisement for the romance of flight."

"He certainly dressed the part."

"That he did."

"I think I'm not alone in saying that when I came into that hangar and saw him standing there, I said to myself, 'This is a guy who can teach me to fly.'"

"With the one mistake of repeating a joke, he became a windbag, nothing but a gag man, and not a good one."

"And we began asking ourselves, 'Am I really going to trust this clown to teach me how to fly? I mean, what if a situation arises in which there's nothing to prevent flying from turning into crashing but what Rudolph Derringer, Certified Fucking Idiot, has taught me?'"

"He crashed."

"One little mistake, and he crashed."

"Let that be a lesson to you, kid."

"Yeah," I said, trying on, to see how well it fit, their snarling rejection of Rudolph Derringer and trying, behind my back, the method of cupping a hand to hold a cigarette and keep it safe from the rain.

"You going to the course at the library next Wednesday?" one of the men asked.

"What course is that?" asked another.

"Cultivation and Propagation of Succulents."

"I don't know. Maybe."

"They make very nice houseplants, I'm told. It's free, and you get to take a cutting home with you."

"I might be there. How about you, kid?"

"I'm not sure," I said. I patted my pockets as if looking for something. "You know, I think I left my—pen—in the hangar. I've got to go back. Maybe I'll see you next week."

I returned to the hangar and found Derringer slumped in a chair, a pint bottle of Don Q rum in his hand and a distant look on his face.

"Mr. Derringer?" I asked.

"Yeah?" he said without looking at me.

"I was wondering if you'd be willing to give me a few lessons for a reduced price. I've got my own plane. Almost. Well, not a plane exactly. An aerocycle—but it's not quite finished. Maybe I could get by with just three lessons—taking off, steering, and landing. Make that four lessons. There's one other thing that I really want to learn—something I yearn to learn."

"Oh, yeah? What do you *yearn* to learn?"

"I yearn to learn the Immelmann turn."

"What's that?" he asked.

"It's—it's—well—"

"Yeah?"

"It's on page eighty-eight," I said, pointing to his copy of *Elements of Aeronautics.*

He flipped the book open and flipped the pages until he came to page eighty-eight. He bent over the book and studied the diagram. "You must be crazy!" he said. "That looks impossible."

ALTHOUGH I had only that one flying lesson, it did teach me something. I think I can see that I took much of what Derringer said about seat-
of-the-pants flying to heart. I became a seat-of-the-pants flier when I
eventually did build my aerocycle and took off for the Faustroll Institute,
and much later in life, I became a seat-of the-pants memoirist. When you
are a seat-of-the-pants memoirist you don't write about your life; you live
your memoirs. You begin to feel that you and your account of yourself
are one, like a mythical beast.

Chapter 37
If Only . . .

I TIPTOED into Albertine's hospital room, in case she was asleep. She was. She lay on her back, with the bed cranked up so that her upper body was raised from the horizontal. Her mouth hung slightly open. As she breathed, she snuffled. I wouldn't call it snoring, not quite, but it was a near cousin. I wasn't seeing her at her best. The slack mouth and the snuffling did not become her. I knew that the woman who had worried about exposing her underwear in a dogboarding accident would not want me—or anyone else—to see her this way, so I retreated from the room and returned to the nurses' station down the hall.

"She asleep?" asked a nurse.

"Yeah," I said.

"It's the meds. She'll go in and out. You can wait here if you want, but it would be better if you wait in there with her, so she sees you when she wakes up."

"You think so?"

"She's been asking for you."

"She has?" I said. I shouldn't have been surprised to find that she had been asking for me, but I was. I was so pleased and flattered by the thought of her asking for me, like a wasting heroine in a sentimental movie, that I may have blushed and stammered. In fact, I'm sure I did. I didn't say, "She has?" I said, "Sh-sh-she has?"

The nurse gave me a smile and said, "Of course she has. You know she has." There was something in her manner, and her smile, that made me wonder if she thought that I wasn't really Albertine's husband. "You ought to wait in her room—so that you're there when she wakes up."

"Yes," I said. "I'll do that."

I returned to her room and found her awake.

"Hi," she said shyly, as if we didn't know each other as well as we do.

"Hi," said I, in much the same manner. Perhaps it was the setting that made us feel unfamiliar.

"Did you write about the crash?" she asked, with a bit of vacancy at the end, as if she had omitted *yet*.

"Yes," I said. "I set it in Central Park."

"A much nicer setting," she said. "Much nicer. But why there? Why did you put us there?"

"I had you crash into a dogboarder instead of a construction worker."

"I can't stand those dogboarders."

"I know."

"Did you include the flying EMTs?"

"What?"

"The flying EMTs. When I was in the emergency room, there were EMTs who brought people in by helicopter. They landed on the roof."

"I forgot."

"They were dashing. They had a certain swagger."

"I'll put them in," I promised.

"Thank you," she said, shy again.

"I wish it hadn't happened," I said. "I wish we could take the day back, and choose to do something else instead of riding—"

"—in the park."

"Yeah," I said.

"So do I," she said. "Believe me."

"I'm sure you do," I said.

"Yes," she said, "I suppose so, but that sort of regret can lead you down the dark alleys of If and into the dangerous part of town they call If Only."

Chapter 38
Recruiting the Crew

I KNEW—or I thought I knew—that I could count on certain people to help me when I actually began to build the aerocycle. I thought that I could count on my friends, and I thought I knew who they were. As I began letting them know that the big day was nearly upon us, however, I began to hear from them a chorus of excuses. Actually, it wasn't a chorus, since their excuses were all highly individual and sometimes quite inventive; it was more like a cacophony of excuses.

Raskol announced that he was spending all his time cramming for the dread-inducing College Competency Exams, the CCEs, though he had often told me that he considered college a waste of time and wanted to go to work on the bay after he finished high school, eventually buy his own boat, and live a life much like his father's. "I'm working with a tutor," he said with apparent pride. "Rudolph Derringer."

"CFI?" I asked.

"Huh?" he said.

"Never mind," I said.

Spike O'Grady claimed to have become a balletomane. "I can't miss any of the performances during the Babbington Festival of the Dance," she said swooningly.

"I didn't even know there was a Babbington Festival of the Dance," I admitted.

With an expression of wonder at my ignorance, she said, "It's an annual affair."

I shrugged.

"All those darling children from Miss Lois's School of Dance and Ar-
lene's Dancing Academy and all the other little dancing schools in the
greater Babbington area hold their recitals in one enchanting festival," she
said, cracking her knuckles.

Margot and Martha Glynn claimed that they had to spend every waking hour posing for their father, the painter Andy Glynn. "Our father is
having a bit of a *crise*," said Margot. "He has not been selling quite so
well as he used to."

"And that is putting a pinch on the family finances," said Martha.
"Cheaper cuts of meat, domestic wine, the usual cutbacks."

"But he's begun to worry about the future, and he feels the need to put
some money by for the wife and daughters, in anticipation of the time
when he shuffles off the mortal coil."

"So he's decided to reinvent himself as a painter of frankly erotic
studies of beautiful young girls interpreted as nymphs and fairies," said
Martha.

"You can see that we are kept quite busy," said Margot with a proud
toss of her golden hair.

You may not be surprised, Reader, to learn that I thought then of abandoning the flying project entirely and devoting myself to assisting Andy
Glynn, but I was stung by the girls' apparently giving not a thought to the
idea of abandoning the erotic painting project and assisting me, so I just
said, "Yes, I guess you are," and went to browse in greener pastures.

When I asked Mr. MacPherson what he thought "the mortal coil" was,
he said, "The mortal coil is a lot like the madding crowd or the vale of
tears. It's where we live, and it's the condition of human life, with its
worries and woes, hustle and bustle, turmoil and tumult, which is what
coil means, as perhaps you did not know, and the certainty of death,
which is what *mortal* means, as I suspect you did know. 'Deid men are
free men,' my father used to say. They are free of the coil, at least, and far
from the madding crowd. Hamlet used the 'mortal coil' phrase in his famous soliloquoy, the one that begins with 'To be or not to be: that is the
question.' When he's thinking of killing himself, he wonders what death
would be like. Like sleep? 'To sleep: perchance to dream,' he says, 'ay,
there's the rub; / For in that sleep of death what dreams may come / When
we have shuffled off this mortal coil / Must give us pause.'"

"Would you like to help me build a small airplane out of parts of old motorcycles?" I asked.

"Sorry, Peter," he said. "After school hours, I abandon myself to strong drink."

"Really?" I asked, astonished by such an admission from an adult, and particularly from a teacher.

"'It's a dry tale that disna end in a drink,'" he said.

Marvin Jones claimed that he had to entertain visiting relatives. "My aunt Sylvia and uncle Gordon are coming," he said, "and seven of my cousins. There's a lot of cooking to do, housecleaning, turning the basement into a dormitory, that sort of thing."

"Yeah," I said, "but I thought you'd—"

"Family is the most important thing, Peter. As my mother says, 'Friends may be friends for a lifetime, but family is forever.'"

"Yeah," I said. "But remember that 'Freendship canna stand aye on ane side.'"

"Who said that?"

"Mr. MacPherson."

Matthew Barber claimed that he wanted to help but couldn't because his mother had forbidden it, on the grounds that being associated with "Peter and his crazy flying scheme" would make him a pariah at the Summer Institute. Patti Fiorenza was rarely to be seen. She was either off riding in a convertible with a tattooed thug or rehearsing with whatever doo-wop group she happened to be in at the moment. Porky White said that he was so busy with plans to open a second clam bar that he couldn't even think of anything else.

"I know it doesn't seem like such a big deal to open another little restaurant in the next town, but I've got a feeling that this is the start of something big," he said. "I see Kap'n Klam Family Restaurants from coast to coast someday, and I want to make sure that I get it right, right from the start. You understand, don't you?"

"Sure," I said. "I feel the same way about my solo flight to New Mexico. I'd like to get it right, right from the start—which is going to be hard if I never get the plane built."

"Mm, yeah," he said distractedly. Then he stopped what he was doing, thought for a moment, and said suddenly, with enthusiasm, "Say, Peter!

How about if you trail one of those advertising banners behind you, like the ones you see behind the planes that buzz the beach? 'Kap'n Klam is coming!' It'll get people wondering who the Kap'n is, get them interested in buying a franchise."

"A franchise?"

"Yeah," he said, returning to the papers that were spread across the counter. "It's a brilliant idea. I'll explain it to you later. What do you say about the banner?"

"Okay, I guess, if it's not too heavy."

"How heavy could it be? I'll get to work on it. Sorry I can't help you with the plane."

"Aerocycle."

"Right. Sorry."

MY FRIENDS, it seemed, had let me down. My father, on the other hand, and to my great surprise, was eager. When I returned home, defeated in my effort to rally recruits to the cause, he was out in the garage, making an inventory of the materials on hand and assigning tasks to personnel we didn't have, pausing now and then to rub his hands in anticipatory glee, looking forward to the start of the work.

"Big day tomorrow!" he said when he noticed me.

"Yeah," I said. "Big day."

I didn't have the heart to tell him that we'd be working alone, or to point out that work without help was likely to be work without glee.

Chapter 39
Al and I, Unstoppable

ALBERTINE attempted to shift her position, winced, tried to smile as if the pain she felt were not really so bad, then settled back against the pillow and lay there in silence for a while before she spoke, or before she could manage to speak.

"So he did help you," she said.

"No," I said. "I've made him an enthusiastic supporter of my plans to see how things might have gone between us if he had been an enthusiastic supporter of my plans."

"Peter, did he ever actually *prevent* you from doing the things that you thought were important to you, the things that you thought were worth doing?"

"You've forgotten about his not allowing me to see that play?"

"Other than that."

"He told me that I couldn't change my major to molluscan biology."

"But you did."

"He told me that I couldn't marry you."

"So did your mother."

"True."

"And yet you did."

"I was unstoppable. So were you. Your parents offered you Europe to reject me, remember."

"A trip to Europe, not Europe."

"You mean—you had your price—but they wouldn't meet it?"

"Nothing short of all of Europe would have stopped me."

Chapter 40
I, Panmuphle

TO DISTRACT MYSELF from feelings of bitterness and betrayal, I decided to make another try at my translation of the *Adventures & Opinions of Doctor Faustroll, Pataphysician*. Reading what I had done, I felt that I understood Panmuphle's frustration at being unable even to locate the dilatory tenant of the Bonhommes, felt it at a level deeper than the words on the page. It resembled, I saw on rereading, my frustration at being unable to find a friend when I needed one. I also saw that Monsieur Jarry—as I thought of him in my schoolboy way—intended Panmuphle to be ridiculous. He was officious with regard to the duties of his office, jealous of its perquisites, and vigorous in his efforts to avoid blame. He was a petty bureaucrat, a type of being my father often railed against at the dinner table. I began trying to plod through what I had done, word for word, but the more I worked, the more clearly I could see in my mind's eye the interview between Panmuphle and the mayor of Paris when the bumbling bailiff returned in defeat and began to make his excuses. I found myself straying from the letter of the text to what I took to be the spirit, and I produced this:

The mayor's door stood partly open, as it ordinarily does when he is at work within. I knocked with due deference, employing the modest tap that my dear wife did me the honor of referring to as "the badge of my diplomatism" when I demonstrated it for her. After a moment's pause, during which I detected no response to my knock from monsieur le mayor, I peered discreetly around the frame of the door, knocked again, cleared my throat, and said, as a request that he acknowledge and admit me, "Monsieur le Mayor?"

Employing that gruff tone that he affects to hide from others the avuncular affection he feels for me, he asked, "What is it now, Panmuphle?"

"Sir," I said, "today I have—"

"Today?" he said, raising his head from his work and regarding me with querulous eyes. "What day is today?"

"It is the eighth of February, sir." He made no response, but his eyes seemed to grow more querulous. "In the year eighteen hundred ninety-eight," I added.

With an economical gesture of the hand, he indicated that I should proceed.

"Today I have been frustrated in my attempt to do my duty, sir."

"Then today is a day like all days, is it not?" he said, attempting through this drollery to put me at my ease.

"Yes, thank you, sir," I said, with a smile to show that I understood his humorous intent. "The source of my frustration, sir, is my inability to locate a certain Dr. Faustroll."

"Faustroll? Faustroll?" he muttered.

"Yes, sir. He is the tenant, or perhaps the lodger, of Mr. and Mrs. Jacques Bonhomme, owners of a house situated at 100 Richer Street."

"Yes?"

"Yes. They appealed to me, sir, as the elected member for the district."

"Mm."

"Dr. Faustroll—if indeed he has the right to the apellation—owes to the Bonhommes the sum of three hundred seventy-two thousand francs and 27 centimes, for eleven terms of rent on the premises annexed to the Bonhomme house and numbered 100 bis."

"Mm."

"I made my way to Richer Street, sir, and found the lodgings of Dr. Faustroll."

"You are certain of that?"

"But yes, Monsieur le Mayor. The number 100 was clearly marked on the house."

"And you were in the correct street?"

"Monsieur—"

"Go on, go on."

"I rang the bell, I knocked, and I called the name of Dr. Faustroll."

"And getting no response, you left, I suppose."

"For lunch, yes, but I returned following my lunch, and again I rang the bell, again I knocked, and again I called the name of Dr. Faustroll. Again and again."

"No one came to the door, I suppose."

"No one."

"Forgive me, Panmuphle, but you are certain that you were knocking at the door of the residence of Dr. Faustroll?"

"I interrogated the neighbors, sir, and they declared to me that it was indeed the residence of Dr. Faustroll."

"Had you prepared a Commandment in accordance with article 819 of the Code of Civil Procedure?"

"Yes, sir. I had, sir." I unrolled the Commandment and displayed it, but he did not look up from the papers on his desk. "I put considerable effort into it, and into the two copies," I said. "Notice the care I've taken with the lettering—"

"Panmuphle," he said with a sigh betraying the weight of his office, "why did you not have some relative or neighbor of Dr. Faustroll sign the original and take a copy to present to Faustroll when he returned?"

"Sir, I could not find anyone who was willing to do that. There were no relatives of Faustroll's there, nor any servants, and none of the neighbors was willing to assume the duty of signing my original and being presented with the copy." I paused for a moment. The account of my struggles had left me a bit breathless. "I was uncertain, sir, what my next action ought to be, so I returned here immediately to speak with you personally, seeking your advice and counsel."

"Is the Commandment properly worded?"

"But of course, sir," I said, and, to prove that it was so, I began to read the Commandment to him: " 'I, René-Isidore Panmuphle, *et cetera,* hereby make Commandment, *et cetera,* to Mr. Faustroll, doctor, *et cetera,* within a period of time not to exceed twenty-four hours to pay to the plaintiff, *et cetera,* the sum of three hundred seventy-two thousand francs and 27 centimes, *et cetera,* declaring to him that failing to satisfy, *et cetera*—' "

"All right, all right, *et cetera,*" he growled in his collegial way. "Let me have it."

I laid the original before him and he signed it with a flourish. "Leave a copy at Faustroll's residence," he said.

"Yes, sir."

"Nail it to the door if you must."

"Certainly."

"And see that the proper stamps are affixed to it."

"Of course, sir," I said, backing out the door. "Thank you, sir."

While I was at work on this version of the very first part of the *Adventures & Opinions of Doctor Faustroll, Pataphysician,* I experienced the realization—a realization accompanied by a great deal of pleasure—that I was doing something like flying: I had taken off from the original and had embarked on a flight of fancy. I could not help but think about what Mr. MacPherson had said earlier: "If they set you the task of writing a dissertation, perhaps you'll choose to do it on the question of whether an imaginary solution can be built from scratch, from whole cloth, or must needs be built from a kit, a set of precut pieces that we cut as we live, without even noticing that we're doing the work." I was working from a kit, a set of precut pieces, and I was acutely aware of my having done the work of making the pieces over all the years that had preceded my taking off.

Chapter 41
The Boss Takes His Place

ON THE MORNING OF THE DAY when my father and I were to begin building the aerocycle, alone, I was reluctant to get out of bed. I could hear my father downstairs, whistling, as he did whenever a burst of enthusiasm came over him and he felt for a while as if he were a boy again, feeling the boyish lift of possibility in his life. I was as reluctant to join my father in building the aerocycle as I was to join him in his enthusiasm. I found enthusiasm unseemly in him. Recalling that morning and the feelings that kept me in bed, I think that I may at the time have found enthusiasm unseemly in any adult. From the point of view of my teenage self, adults didn't wear enthusiasm well. Seeing them under the influence of enthusiasm was like seeing them drunk and telling jokes. From my point of view, my tipsy parents embarrassed themselves in attempting to be funny, and the next morning they seemed to realize that they had. I thought that they should also have realized that they embarrassed themselves in attempting to recover their youthful enthusiasm. I know that I was embarrassed for my father when I saw the signs of his enthusiasm — his whistling and bustling and the fraternal attitude that he took toward me when the fit was on him, as if we had always been great friends and he had never been the Grand Naysayer.

Hiding from my father's enthusiasm wasn't my only reason for lingering in bed. I was also giving my friends time to gather secretly to surprise me. I nursed the slim hope that they had conspired to play a joke on me. If that were the case, then they must now be gathering outside, or in the garage, preparing to surprise me when I came down to begin work. I wanted to give them plenty of time to gather so that the slugabeds and stragglers among them wouldn't miss seeing my look of surprise and gratitude when I discovered that they were all there to help me, that they were friends indeed. The moment promised to be poignant and exhilarating, with lots of backslapping and hugging and many lumpy throats. I didn't want anybody to miss it. I strained to hear any sound that might betray their secret assembly, but I couldn't hear a thing. Evidently, they were a stealthy bunch, those friends of mine.

Then I heard footsteps—but not outside, where the sound of the footsteps of my gathering friends would have come from. They were footsteps inside the house, footsteps approaching the foot of the stairs, and they were my father's footsteps.

Then: "Peter!"

From me, reluctantly: "Yeah?"

"Time to get going! Sooner begun is sooner done!"

"Have you been talking to Mr. MacPherson?" I groaned.

"I—um—" he began, and then he added, "I—ah—who?"

"Never mind," I said. "I'm getting up."

I got up. I dressed. I brushed my teeth. I shaved. (Wait a minute. That can't be right. I wasn't shaving yet. Or was I? This was just before the end of my junior year in high school. Because I had started kindergarten early and skipped the third grade, I was only fifteen. Was I shaving? Now that I think about it, I believe that I was, perhaps as often as monthly. Maybe I did shave that morning, mindful that someone might take commemorative snapshots.)

I dawdled through breakfast, stretching it out and stretching it out, until, finally, there was nothing to do but get up and go out to the garage. My friends were not there, but my father was, bustling about. He had already scratched a sketch of the wing framework in the sand that served as the floor of the garage and laid a few lengths of aluminum tubing in place on the sketch. That should have been my work. I wondered whether he had gotten it right.

"How's it going?" I asked.

"Great! Just great!" he claimed.

"What do you want me to do?"

"Hey, I'm not the boss here," he said, incredibly. "This is your project, your baby, your dream. You tell me what you want me to do."

I asked myself whether he could possibly mean that. Was he really there to help me? Or was he there, as he usually was, to tell me that what I was doing, or what I wanted to do, was wrong, that he knew a better way, the only way, his way? I decided to find out.

"Okay," I said. "Let me see that sketch."

He gave it to me. With my sketch in hand, I began walking the perimeter of his version, his lines drawn in the sand, making corrections. I could almost hear him bristling, but I didn't care or dare to look up to see whether he was fuming at my impudence in changing what he had done. I kept my attention strictly on the work of making the template on the floor match the sketch. When I had finished, and only then, I raised my head to look at him, to see how he had taken my treating him as he had always treated me, correcting his work without asking, altering it as I thought it should be altered, and that was when I saw that we were not alone. Behind my father, just outside the garage door, was quite a crowd. Everyone I had asked to help was there, and many more, including Mr. MacPherson, who immediately snatched the sketch from me and went around the template again, correcting my corrections. All my friends were there, and a lump began to form in my throat, as I had known it would.

"Hey, Pete," said Spike, "whatcha doin'?"

I swallowed hard and said, as nonchalantly as I could, "Building an aerocycle."

"Oh, right! I remember you mentioned that. Mind if we help?"

"No," I said as if the idea had never occurred to me. "I don't mind."

"All right, everyone!" said Mr. MacPherson. "The surprise portion of the event is over. I'm sure we can all see that our little stunt was a great success and Peter is deeply moved by our demonstration of loyalty. Now it's time to get to work. I want this machine to fly in forty-eight hours. Line up to my right and I'll assign tasks based on ability and experience."

People began lining up. I didn't see any reason to join them. After all, I was the boss.

"Peter?" said Mr. MacPherson with a gesture toward the end of the line. It would have been useless to object. I took my place with the others.

"Mr. Leroy?" said Mr. MacPherson, looking over his glasses at my father.

"I was already working—" he began, but Mr. MacPherson's stare was enough to silence him. He fell into line behind me.

It was an awkward moment for both of us, shuffling along at the end of the line, awaiting assignments on my project in his garage. After a long, silent minute, my father said, "You have a lot of friends."

"Yeah," I said.

"I envy you that," he said.

Chapter 42
Flyguys

AS I APPROACHED Albertine's hospital room the next evening, I could hear her humming. It was as unmistakable a sign of enthusiasm in her as whistling had been in my father.

"You sound chipper," I said as I leaned over to kiss her.

"Oh, I am. If only I could get out of here, I think I'd be quite chipper indeed."

"Any word on that?"

"It's hard to pin anyone down."

"Are you feeling better?"

"I still can't turn at all. The pain is just too much."

"I'm sorry—"

"And the lump on the side of my head is as big as a grapefruit—half a grapefruit."

"Your hair hides it."

"I know, but it worries me."

"I'm sure."

"However . . . I can sit at the side of the bed and I can stand with the walker." She inclined her head toward a framework of aluminum tubing that stood beside the bed, a "walker" that allowed a person to stand within it and support herself by taking her weight partially on her arms, with her hands gripping plastic foam pads on the uppermost part of the frame.

"Really?" I said. That seemed like tremendous progress to me.

"Yes. Really. Apparently I have to pass a test to get out of here."

"A test?"

"The Walker Test."

"You have to show that you can use it?"

"I have to show that I can go some distance using it."

"How far?"

"There's some disagreement about that. The big nurse says a hundred feet, but the flyguys say a hundred yards. Of course, they may be pulling my leg—"

"The 'flyguys'?"

"That's what they call themselves. The EMTs who fly the helicopters."

"Oh."

"They're so cute."

"I'll bet."

"They've got swagger."

"You've mentioned that."

"I have?"

"Yes. The other evening."

"Oh? I don't remember. It must be the pain medication. Do I smell something good?"

"I brought chicken tikka masala." Albertine is fond of chicken prepared in a hundred ways, and chicken tikka masala is at or near the top of the list.

"I don't have much of an appetite."

"Did you eat the hospital dinner?"

"The flyguys brought me a hero."

"A hero?"

"Italian cold cuts."

"You ate a whole hero?"

"No, no. Just a couple of bites. But that couple of bites filled me right up."

We talked about coincidence and accident for a while, but it was a conversation in fits and starts. Al was still sleepy, inclined to close her eyes after a few minutes, doze for a while, then wake and smile in apology for having drifted away. When she was awake, we talked, and when she was asleep, I ate a little of the chicken.

AFTER LEAVING ALBERTINE, I detoured to the emergency room instead of going straight home. The emergency "room" was actually a suite of rooms arranged around a central administrative and bureaucratic area that was open except for a chest-high partition defining it and limiting its access to two openings. A dozen seats were arranged opposite one of the openings, provided for those who accompanied the ill and injured to the emergency room, and I sat in one of them, choosing the same one that I had occupied on the night of Albertine's crash, when I had waited for her there while she was being examined elsewhere in the building. Now I had come to the emergency room because I wanted to see what the flying EMTs, the flyguys, looked like. There were none in evidence when I arrived, so I waited, but I feared that I might be told to leave before I got the chance to see them. I expected to be challenged about my right to be in the emergency room, occupying a seat provided for the companion to an ailing party when I had no ailing party to play companion to, but no challenge ever came. I was never asked to move along, never told to leave. No one seemed to notice me at all. I could have sat there all night, I think. I might have sat there every night. The thought came to me that sitting there for a while every night might be interesting to try, to see whether anyone ever noticed that I didn't belong there, that I had no legitimate claim to one of the molded seats. It might also be possible to get free coffee that way.

A phone rang, and its ringing occasioned a sudden bustle and flutter that had not occurred when other phones rang. Someone sprang up to answer it, and I saw that the ringing phone was red, mounted on a pillar at the very center of the central bureaucratic area.

"Schurz ER," said the young woman who answered it. She flipped a switch beside the phone, and the incoming side of the conversation was broadcast to all of us. What we heard was a man's voice, stern, clipped, efficient, self-confident, calling from a helicopter on its way to Schurz from the scene of an accident somewhere, calling out over the roar of engine and wind. (Schurz, I learned later, was the "catchment" hospital for trauma cases in a wide area roughly centered on our neighborhood. Three helicopter EMT services transported victims to Schurz, landing on a helipad on the roof of the hospital, where the flyguys offloaded the injured, commandeered an elevator, and rushed their charges to the ER.)

The voice detailed the nature and extent of injuries sustained in a motorcycle accident by a male Caucasian who would be arriving at the ER soon, and three people—a doctor and two nurses, I think—began preparing a bed and assembling equipment. After what seemed only a moment, double doors burst open down a hallway to my right and two flyguys came through, wheeling a collapsible stretcher with a victim on it. The flying EMTs were suited up in jumpsuits, gray with a red lightning bolt over their breast pockets and a much larger red lightning bolt on the back with the name MEDAIR beneath it. They were all business, those flyguys. They were professional. They were cool. They did not smile . . . but they sure did swagger.

Chapter 43
Albertine on Coincidence and Accident

AT HOME, in bed, alone, missing Albertine, aching for her, I brought her to mind and rehearsed our conversation on coincidence and accident.

"You won't believe this," she had said, drifting up from sleep to a state of drowsy wakefulness, "but one of the flyguys is the grandson of your Mr. MacPherson."

"What a coincidence," I remarked.

"He asked me if I planned to sue," she added matter-of-factly.

I stopped eating the chicken tikka masala, closed the lid of the container, and asked, "Sue?"

"Mmm," she said distantly.

"You seem to be in a wee bit of a dwam," I said, as Mr. MacPherson might have.

"Mmm," she reiterated.

"Are you?"

"In a dwam?"

"Planning to sue."

"No. My crash was an accident."

"Pure and simple?"

"Of course not," she said, suddenly more alert. "Why do we say that? 'Pure and simple?'" Then, because she recognized that the question might have been asked by Mr. MacPherson himself, she spoke in an amusing version of his brogue. "Is anything ever pure and simple? No. Nothing. Everything is impure and complex. I suppose we say 'pure and simple' because we wish that something would be pure and simple, we

yearn for things that are pure and simple, things that are pure enough and
simple enough for us to understand them, see through them like pure water and swallow them as easily as simple syrup—but nothing is ever pure
and simple."

"You're right," I said. "Your crash was an accident, but forget the pure
and simple part."

"Am I raving?" she asked.

"Not exactly."

"It must be the pain medication."

"Maybe you should rest again."

"I think I'd like to make a point about the concepts of coincidence and
accident, if I can stay awake long enough."

"Please do."

"Feel free to eat while I ramble."

"That's okay. While you talk, I listen. While you sleep, I eat."

"Coincidence," she began, and I could see from the way she paused and
puckered her lips and knit her brows that she had not prepared this in advance, "is a simple matter of the simultaneous occurrence of two events."

"'Simple'?"

"You said, 'While you talk, I listen.'"

"I forgot myself."

"Eat the chicken—and don't talk with your mouth full."

"Yes, dear."

"Oooh," she said suddenly, and she shivered.

"What's the matter?"

"A chill," she said, "as if the ghosts of Einstein and Gödel just passed
through the room, admonishing me as they wandered through against
playing fast and loose with time and simultaneity."

"Oh," I said, and I couldn't keep myself from glancing around, trying
to catch a glimpse of the famous friends.

"I know better than to claim that simultaneity is universal and abso-
lute," she assured them, "but I'm only discussing the type of accident that
is local and macroscopic, on the level where daily life is lived, the level
where collisions with dogboarders occur. There—or here—as the term
accident is usually used—make that commonly used—an accident is an

unfortunate coincidence," she said firmly, in the manner of one who will brook no further interruption. "The idea of misfortune is so embedded in the term that on the rare occasions when we want to use it to designate a coincidence that brings good fortune, we have to specify that we mean a 'happy accident.' If your Mr. MacPherson were here, Peter, he would tell you that at its Latin root, *accident* simply means 'occurrence' or 'what has befallen.' After the fact, we ascribe significance to the simultaneity, sometimes great significance, based on the effect that one of the simultaneous occurrences has had on us, and so we give to coincidence a meaning that in most cases it ought not to have. That habit of overestimating the importance of coincidence has driven coincidence to its low status among skeptics. The truth is that coincidence is not merely commonplace but constant, a pervasive fact of life and all existence. The universal characteristic of the vast panorama of 'it all' is ceaseless motion, an uncountable number of events, happening all the time, with an uncountable number of them occurring coincidentally at any moment. We regard those events as directionless and meaningless until one of them affects us. At that moment, or slightly later, after the brain has done its work, we interpret all the other events in the light of that one that has affected us. That one is significant to us *because* it has affected us, and in our worldview we are always at the center of all action. No occurrence becomes significant until or unless it affects us. Put another way, we could say that an event will become significant *when* or *if* it affects us, but not until or unless it does. So, most of everything that happens is taken by the human mind to be insignificant, but the little bit that directly affects us we take to be tremendously significant, looming large over all the rest, and we suddenly seem to see an astonishing coincidence or set of coincidences that produced the significant event. If we could ever understand at a deep level the essential insignificance of simultaneity, we would not have our cultural fascination with the fallacy of significant coincidence." She was beginning to fade, and she knew it. She gave me a wan smile, as if apologizing in advance for the drifting off she was about to do. "I said 'cultural fascination,' but maybe our fascination is even deeper than that," she continued bravely. "It may even be genetic. Apparently, according to the reading I've been doing, one of the brain's primary functions is the detection of coincidence. Certain structures—combinations of synaptic links among neurons—work as coincidence detectors. Detecting coincidence must be of such high evolutionary value that it became a part of our genetic makeup . . . long . . . long . . . ago."

Visiting hours were over, and of the chicken tikka masala only a snack was left.

"Do you want me to leave this with you?" I asked. "One of the nurses can probably heat it up."

"No," she said drowsily. "Thank you. You have it for breakfast."

"I will," I said. "Good night, my darling." We kissed, and as she dwammed over I left her for the night.

Chapter 44
The Spirit of Camaraderie

When energy is converted from one kind into another, no energy is actually destroyed. We may lose track of it, but it exists in some form. The statement of this fact is called the Law of the Conservation of Energy.

Francis Pope and Arthur S. Otis
Elements of Aeronautics

IMPRACTICAL CRAFTSMAN had told the truth, at least in part: the aerocycle could be built in a single weekend, and I think that it could have been built, or at least assembled, within the confines of the family garage. However, the crafty folks at *IC* had neglected to say how many people they expected to work on the construction. They never wrote in terms of builder hours. If you had a gang on the job, as I did, the aerocycle could be built in a single weekend. I am not really qualified to assess the adequacy of the confines of the family garage for the complete construction of an aerocycle, because not all of the work on my aerocycle was done there. We subcontracted some of it.

We built the plane during a time in Babbington when everyone knew how to do something, or at least knew somebody who knew how to do something, so we had a network of artisans available to us, if we knew who they were and how to enlist them. Mr. MacPherson, brilliant in the role of the boss, was quick to notice when a task was beyond the ken of the worker he had assigned to it. He had a sharp eye for the telltale signs: the befuddled brow; the perplexed scratching of the head; the first clumsy, hesitant effort; the furtive glance that followed a mistake and betrayed the intention to let it go uncorrected if it had gone unnoticed. As soon as he saw any evidence of befuddlement or perplexity or clumsiness or carelessness, he would seek someone better qualified, asking, for example, "Does anyone among those of you here assembled know someone with a drill press and the skill to use it?"

Someone always did, and so the most difficult and exacting tasks were sent to shops—or, sometimes, to family garages—around town, shuttled there and back by car or bicycle, even on foot. This subcontracting would certainly have resulted in chaos and idleness, with many willing workers—those who had been assigned to assemble the aluminum skeleton of the wings, for example—left behind in the garage, finding that they had nothing to do while the components essential to their work were across town being drilled by somebody's uncle—had it not been for Spike, whom Mr. MacPherson had immediately appointed his assistant, in charge of keeping idleness and chaos at bay. She created on the fly a chart that tracked every outsourced job, and she assigned a tracking agent to each of those jobs whose sole function was to observe the progress of the work and report to her. With up-to-the-minute knowledge of the state of readiness of every component and subcomponent, she was able to predict when the item would arrive and to ensure that a group gathered just in time to unload it and begin incorporating it in the grand scheme.

"Rose," said Mr. MacPherson suddenly while watching Raskol, Marvin, and me wrestling with the tricky job of fabricating the framework that would hold the engine in front of the handlebars, "how long will it be before the tail assembly is delivered?"

"My best estimate is ninety-seven minutes, Mr. Mac," Spike said with a glance at her watch and clipboard, "but remember that it won't have the fabric on it."

"Mm. I had forgotten that. Are we going to have to send it out again?"

"I don't think so. I've got Patti Fiorenza out scouring the town for people with upholstery experience, and I'm hoping we'll be able to get them in here to cut, fit, and stitch the fabric right on the frame."

"Good thinking."

"Thanks."

"But how is Patti getting around? She's not going to be able to cover much of the town on foot. Perhaps the telephone—"

"Rocco is driving her around in his T-bucket."

"What on earth is that, Rose?"

"It's a hot rod, sir."

"I see. A hot rod. I understand the use of *hot,* meaning 'powerful and keen to go,' as *fiery* does in 'a fiery steed,' but I wonder why *rod* should be the word for the steed itself."

"Possibly a corruption of *ride,* sir," suggested Spike.

Mr. MacPherson looked at her with love-light in his eyes. "Quite possibly so, Rose," he said. "Quite possibly so. Did you arrange for that transportation?"

"I can't take the credit, sir. Rocco found Patti's prominent breasts and buttocks, attractively displayed in a tight top and tighter skirt, a powerful incentive to drive her anywhere she might want to go. That's why I chose her for the job."

"You are a smart cookie, Rose."

"Thank you, sir."

They knit their brows in tandem, wondering about that use of *cookie.*

I WOULD BE less than generous if I did not acknowledge here that Mr. MacPherson and Spike were not the only ones who kept the crew occupied and available during what might otherwise have been downtime. Some of the credit has to go to my father, who put them to work mowing the lawn and weeding the vegetable garden.

TO ALL OF US but Spike and Mr. MacPherson, I think, our efforts truly did seem chaotic. We did the jobs we were told to do, and we derived some sense of satisfaction from whatever work we were doing, and we were held together in our work by the camaraderie that inevitably binds people who are working in a suburban garage to achieve a great goal, a feeling familiar to any reader who has launched a high-tech start-up, but individually we often had no clear notion of the part that our bit of work was to play in the grand scheme. This, I think, represented a failure in Mr. MacPherson's management style, which was otherwise both masterly and masterful. Even I, who had been dreaming over the drawings of the aero-cycle for weeks, who had a picture of the completed aerocycle ever in my mind's eye, sometimes wasn't sure where the gizmo I had been assigned to assemble would fit in the finished plane, and I think Eddie Granger, who lived a block away from me and was notorious for having brought a teddy bear to school with him in the third grade, may have suffered some permanent damage to his self-esteem when he found himself, after the craft had been assembled and wheeled into the sunlight, left holding the device he had labored on for nearly the entire two days, something that fit nowhere at all in the finished plane but belonged in the sliding assembly of a hideaway ironing board that had been presented as a project for the amateur builder in the same issue of *Impractical Craftsman* as the aerocy-cle, the plans for which had somehow—perhaps by accident—found their way into the chaos of the garage.

ON MANY MORNINGS in Babbington, fog lies along the estuarial stretch of the Bolotomy, a "patchy" fog that is thick in some places, thin in others, obscuring and revealing, so that the landscape and townscape beyond it appear in bits and pieces, like the pieces of a picture puzzle with soft, blurred edges. For quite a while, the workers' understanding of the aerocycle was a similarly patchy picture obscured by a patchy fog. How-ever, the fog began to dissipate, as morning fog does, when the sub-sub-assemblies became subassemblies and the subassemblies began to come together as assemblies, and we began to see not just nameless parts whose functions we couldn't describe or predict, but wings, a fuselage, a tail, the motorcycle's running gear, the engine, and, at last, a hybrid machine, part plane, part bike, the aerocycle of my daydreams, my ride to the Land of Enchantment.

I WAS ABOUT TO MOUNT the aerocycle when Rocco, Patti Fiorenza's hot-rodding boyfriend, stepped forward and stayed my progress with a callused hand. I'm proud to say that I didn't flinch.

I did raise an eyebrow questioningly.

"Hey, ah, just a minute, there, Pete," he said, spitting my name's initial plosive at me.

I elevated the eyebrow a notch.

"Somebody left an old rag on the tail there," he said, with a nod in that direction. "Lemme get it off for ya."

He swaggered to the tail and whisked the rag away.

"Jeez," he said. "Look at that."

Painted on the tail was SPIRIT OF BABBINGTON.

A lump formed in my throat. "Is that—your handiwork?" I asked, swallowing.

"Yeah," he said, scuffling his feet and looking at his shoes. "I got a little talent in that area."

"Thanks, Rocco," I said.

"Aaaaa, it's nuttin'," he said. "Patti made me do it."

I gave him a comradely punch on the shoulder, and he gripped my hand in a way that made me think he might break my wrist just for the hell of it, but instead he gave me a return punch.

I mounted the aerocycle without rubbing my shoulder or even betraying a desire or need to rub my shoulder. "Next Saturday," I said. "I'll take off next Saturday."

Chapter 45
Through the Agency of Dust

Coördination is the soul of flying.
  Francis Pope and Arthur S. Otis
  Elements of Aeronautics

I KEEP MY OLD COPY of *Elements of Aeronautics* in the bookcase directly in front of me, on a shelf just above my computer screen. I keep it, and keep it near, not only because it is indispensable as a reference work but because it is a means of transportation: it takes me back. This morning, here and now, with Albertine still in the hospital, just down the street but so far away, the apartment is quiet, empty, and lonely. I've been escaping the loneliness by flipping through the old book and reading at random. A moment ago I returned in memory to the time when I first opened the book, and the pleasure of being back there, back then quivered along my spine. For an instant, I was in my father's bedroom in my grandparents' house, where I slept whenever I visited them. Having returned so completely to a moment in the past, I felt a comforting sense of removal to a safe place. The safest place of all is nowhere, and the past is a place close to that, because as soon as a moment becomes something to remember, it no longer exists for us as anything *but* a moment to remember. The past has had its effect on the present, but the present and its problems can never have an effect on the past, can never find their way there, nor cause any trouble there. We can't go there, either, of course, and yet we experience, from time to time, moments when we seem to have made our way there, to be for a moment where we were rather than where we are. How do we do that? We require an agent. Dust does it for me, the particulate matter of the past. According to Freeman Dyson,

> The dualistic interpretation of quantum mechanics says that the classical world is a world of facts while the quantum world is a world of probabilities. Quantum mechanics predicts what is likely to happen while classical mechanics records what did happen. This division of the world was invented by Niels Bohr, the great contemporary of Einstein who presided over the birth of quantum mechanics. Lawrence Bragg, another great contemporary, expressed Bohr's idea more simply: "Everything in the future is a wave, everything in the past is a particle."

Preserved in my copy of *Elements of Aeronautics* is some dust, some of the dust from the cabinet of wonders in my father's room, a vast number of tiny particles of the past. That dust takes me back—but it hasn't the power to keep me there for long.

My moment in the past, begun when I began this chapter, has nearly run its course; the sensation of actually being there is fading as I write about it, my hasty fingers stumbling over one another. When the feeling was at its strongest, I could smell again the old wood in my father's childhood bedroom, the peculiar and singular smell of the half-completed model airplanes that were stored forever in a cupboard with sliding doors.

At the time, I equated the aroma with loss.

I spoke to my father about this, once upon a time.

"That aroma," I said, one evening when Albertine and I were visiting, probably—though I'm not certain that this is so—for a holiday dinner, "the smell inside that cabinet, where your old airplane models were, somehow it meant loss to me."

"Hmm?"

"Because it was the aroma of the past, of something old and even dead, it meant loss to me, but now, in memory, it means something different from that."

"Mm."

"That aroma was a real thing, you know, particulate matter. It was significant dust. Dust: the only tangible, detectable remnant of the past. One of the ways I knew those unfinished models was through the particulate matter that I inhaled when I opened the cabinet. I smelled them."

"Yeah."

"And the olfactory experience modified the synaptic network in my brain in such a way that the potential for the return of the memory of the smell of that cabinet and the potential for the return of a certain emotion that I felt in that room when I opened that cabinet and examined those models was equal. See what I mean?"

"No."

"The two things—the memory and the emotion—had a high probability of recurring together, and since that time they have recurred together, now and then, apparently coincidentally, and the aroma of old balsa wood and dust is now equated or closely associated not with loss but with comfort and security."

"Oh."

"There's another thing—"

"I figured," he said. "Do you want a beer?"

"Okay."

"You mind getting it?"

"No. Of course not."

"Get me one, too, will you?"

"Sure."

I got us a couple of beers.

"The other thing," I said, "is that the remembered aroma of balsa wood and dust brought back my—um—reverent attitude toward those models. I handled them like cult objects, fetishes. Why did I have that attitude?"

"I don't know."

"I think—but I recognize that this is my adult self thinking—I think that I understood that those models, or more precisely the incompleteness of those models, represented the end of your childhood, and in understanding that your childhood had had an end, had come to an end, I understood that a day would come when mine would end, when I would begin to become someone more like you and less like my little self."

"Yeah?" he asked.

"Yeah," I said.

A moment passed. We drank our beer.

"Those weren't my models," he said.

"They weren't?"

"No. They were Buster's."

"Buster's."

"Yeah."

"Oh."

Buster was my father's brother. He had been killed in World War II, the war that was to everyone I knew "the war," the way that "the city" was to everyone I knew New York City and no other.

"I wasn't much for model building," my father confessed. "That kind of thing was too tedious for me. I didn't have the patience for it." This from a man who sat for hours in a chair watching whatever appeared on his television screen. "Buster really went in for it, though. He'd spend whole afternoons at it. He was the patient one."

Chapter 46
Paneling, a Thought Experiment

"IN THAT MOMENT—that moment that was already past as I tried to record it, already lost—every bit of the old sensation was returned to me by memory, and the catalyst was the smell of old wood and glue and dust that wafted from *Elements of Aeronautics* when I opened it. I remembered the cabinet of unfinished airplane models, of course; but I also remembered the clatter of the old typewriter on the built-in desk, which I used every time I was there, turning pulpy canary yellow second sheets onto the platen, because I was forbidden to use the bond paper in the upper drawer; I remembered the rifles that stood upright in a vertical cabinet to the left of the desk; I remembered the chubby, tubby ship model to the right of the desk, its hull painted orange and white, a lightship, I think; and I remembered the pine paneling on the walls of my father's room, regular and upright, its millwork pattern of ridges and valleys where one panel met the next, and its irregular and intriguing knottiness."

"Mm," said Albertine in a manner disconcertingly like my father's.

"I wonder—I am wondering just now—how much of what I am I owe to the time I spent in that room. I think that as I look back I can see in my life a pattern something like the pattern in the paneling, something in which the irregularity of its knottiness is balanced by the regularity of the millwork."

Her eyes widened.

"The paneling that my father used in my bedroom, when he finally finished, or nearly finished, the corner of the attic in our house in Babbington Heights that became my bedroom, was knotty pine nearly identical to the knotty pine that paneled the walls of his boyhood bedroom. I wonder if I haven't unconsciously or subconsciously patterned my life on that paneling."

Albertine sat in silence for a couple of minutes. Finally, brightening, she said, "You're kidding, right?"

"Kidding?" I asked. "About what?"

"About finding in your past the regularity and irregularity of knotty pine paneling?"

"Um, no."

"Hm."

"What do you mean by that?"

"By what?"

"'Hm.'"

"I think I mean—"

"Mm?"

"I think I mean—"

"Yeah?"

"I think I mean, 'I hope you're not beginning to take yourself too seriously.'"

"Oh."

"You are, aren't you?"

"Possibly. I think it may be the influence of my younger self, the self who was about to take off for the Faustroll Insititute in the Land of Enchantment. Back then, when I had the aerocycle finished, when it was ready and I began to feel that I, too, was ready, that I had become a person who was ready to mount his aerocycle and take off, I began to feel that I had a mission, that perhaps greatness had been thrust upon me."

"It went to your head."

"It did, and I liked it."

"And that was when you began to think of your life as patterned? Milled? Shaped? Shaped, as in shaped by fate, or the Fates?"

"Yes, but knotty, too, remember."

"How long did this last?"

"I don't seem to have gotten over it. Last night I found myself wondering whether I could induce and perhaps sustain that happy state of timelessness if I re-created the childhood conditions that originally inspired it."

"Oh, no."

"If I paneled my workroom with old knotty pine, if I bought some balsa-wood model kits from that dusty hobby shop down the block from us on First Avenue, where all the stock is old, I could assemble them, to a point, and arrange them on shelves where I could see and smell them, and I could work in that paneled room as a happy fool."

"Oh, my dear, my darling, my dreamer," she said, "promise me that you won't actually buy any of that paneling until I get out of here."

"Okay."

"No dusty old model kits, either."

"Okay."

"If I can pass the Walker Test, I can be home tomorrow."

Chapter 47
My Name Stitched in Red

WITH THE AEROCYCLE COMPLETE and waiting in the driveway, and with the announced time of my departure less than a week away, I began to feel important. I began to feel that I stood atop a tower of aviation pioneers, on the shoulders of giants, almost a young giant myself. That feeling may have led eventually to my willingness to have my accomplishment exaggerated by the press and the people of Babbington. In a way, I may have felt that to diminish their perception of my deeds by throwing over them the wet blanket of the truth would be to diminish not only my own daring accomplishment, but the accomplishments of my fellow pioneers as well. I may have felt that. I'm not sure. I offer it in my defense anyway. I know this: I stood taller, I set my jaw more firmly, and I steeled my gaze. I know those things because I checked my stature, my jaw, and my gaze in the hall mirror, frequently. The changes seemed to me to border on the profound, but my mother seemed not to notice. She insisted on helping me pack.

"Mom," I said, drawing myself to my full height, clenching my jaw, whetting my steely gaze, radiating determination and independence, "I'm embarking on a great adventure."

"Oh, I know!" she said. "I'm just as excited as you are. It gives me goose bumps. I should sew name tapes in your underwear."

"Is that something that only mothers can do?" I asked her.

"Sew name tags?" she asked, counting my underwear.

"No. Get from goose bumps to underwear in eight words flat."

"Are you making fun of me?"

"No," I said grumpily, with my eyes down, ashamed of the fact that I had been making fun of her, "it's just that adventurers do not go out into the wide world, braving the unknown, with their names sewn into their underwear."

"They don't?"

"No. They don't."

"How do you know?"

"Mom!"

"Come on, Mr. Smarty Pants. How do you know that the great adventurers haven't 'braved the unknown' with their names sewn into their underwear?"

"I just—"

"Wilbur and Orville Wright."

"Oh, come on."

"They had their names sewn into their underwear."

"How do you know?"

"How do you not?"

"I just—"

"Lucky Lindy."

"He did not have 'Lucky Lindy' sewn into his underwear."

"Of course not. He had 'Charles A. Lindbergh' sewn into his underwear."

"How about Chuck Yeager?" I asked. I thought I had her. I supposed that she did not know who Chuck Yeager was.

"Certainly," she said, a bit uncertainly.

"He had 'Chuck' sewn into his underwear?"

"No, silly," she said, and then she added with a girlish grin, "'Charles Elwood Yeager, Test Pilot.'"

"And those labels were sewn in by his mother?"

"Of course they were sewn in by his mother. Who else?"

"Okay, I give up."

"I'll have them ready in the morning."

SHE DID. The next morning all my underwear, my handkerchiefs, and my socks bore white fabric strips with "Peter Leroy" stitched on them in red thread. They were discreet, and I was grateful for that, but I was surprised to find that I liked them. They had a certain style. I had expected to be embarrassed by them, but I wasn't. My name looked handsome stitched in red. I regretted that there wasn't time for her to add "Birdboy of Babbington," the way Chuck's mother had added "Test Pilot."

Chapter 48
Traveling Light

WHILE TRYING TO PACK the aerocycle, I began to understand what the writers at *Impractical Craftsman* had meant by the assessment that it "would not be practical for long-distance flying." It had not been conceived as a vehicle for cross-country flights. It didn't have room for everything that my mother wanted me to take. It didn't even have room for everything that I wanted to take, and that wasn't half of what my mother wanted me to take. I suppose that the people at *IC* who dreamed up the aerocycle intended it only for what they called "sports use," the sort of flight that wouldn't require a change of clothes, not even a change of underwear, nothing more than buzzing around the neighborhood, never very far from home.

"I don't know how you're going to carry all of this," my mother said, surveying the clothing and gear that we had brought to the driveway, glancing back and forth between the pile of stuff and the two small compartments fitted into the fuselage behind the pilot's seat.

"He can't," said my father. "You've got to start eliminating things."

"Oh, dear," said my mother. She picked up a pair of socks. "Maybe he won't need—" she said, and then, after consideration, "but he will." She put the socks back on the pile and said again, "Oh, dear."

"Mom," I said, putting a hand on her shoulder, "I'm going into unfamiliar territory, but not into 'the great unknown.' You were right to question my calling it that."

"I didn't—"

"Yes, you did. The question—we might even call it a challenge—was in your tone—and you were right. I'm going west, and that's a great adventure, but I'm not the first person to make the trip. Others have preceded me, blazing the trail—"

"What does this have to do—" my father interrupted.

"Because those pioneers preceded me," I pushed on, "there are people out there already. I'm going to travel light, but my resources will be virtually limitless, because I'm going to rely on the kindness of strangers."

"Oh, dear."

"Don't worry, Mom. I'm sure that I'm going to meet wonderful people all along the way, swell people, people who will be happy to take me into their homes, give me a hot supper, tuck me into a warm bed, and send me off with a hearty breakfast."

"I don't know—"

"These are the great American people I'm talking about, Mom, the folk, the salt of the earth. They're not going to turn a wayfarer from their doors. I'm going to put myself at their mercy, arriving as a new pioneer, making his way, asking for the same hospitality that I know you would extend to a boy like me if he arrrived on our doorstep in need."

Her lip trembled. "In need?" she cried.

"Well—not in need exactly—I mean, just needing dinner and a place to stay for the night."

"And a washing machine."

"Right."

"Well, of course we would throw the door wide open, wouldn't we, Bert?"

"Mmmm. I'm not so—" he began, but my mother gave him a look—begging him, I believe, to put himself in the position of a householder finding her son, Peter, on his doorstep, wet, hungry, and miserable, with a cold coming on—and he finished with, "Yeah, I guess."

"And that's what I'm counting on," I said with all the conviction I could dissemble. "I know that when I need food, shelter, and someone to wash my socks, I'll find what I need—out there—by putting my trust in the kind hearts of the good and simple people of this great land."

Most of what I was saying I was quoting from the stirring final scene of *Bitter Harvest of Sour Grapes,* a movie that had played a couple of weeks earlier at the Babbington Theater. In that scene, you may recall, the lanky scion of the destitute Geibe family, their sole hope, decides to change his name to Slim and take to the road as a wandering minstrel and harmonicat, promising to send to his mother, father, and weepy sister all his earnings, withholding only what he needs to keep himself alive and kicking.

"In that case," said my father, pulling things from the pile and stuffing them into the small compartments, "you won't need more than a couple changes of clothing, the first-aid kit, a few hard-boiled eggs, a couple of apples, the compass, the maps, and your rain poncho."

"Oh, dear," said my mother, regarding the great number of things remaining in the pile. "What about—" She reached for my galoshes.

"No, Ella," said my father, laying a restraining hand on hers. "Peter's right. He's got to travel light. Remember that stuff about the American people."

I remember the look on her face. Worry was there, and so was disappointment: she had put a great deal of effort into preparing and assembling all the things she had expected me to take on the journey. In a moment, though, defiance was added to those two emotions. Her eyes darted over the pile of rejected supplies, and I could see that she was determined—desperate, perhaps—to find something that she would be able to add to my gear. Her eyes lit up. "Well!" she cried, springing on the volume of *Faustroll*. "I suppose you'll need this at the Faustroll Institute!"

"I sure will!" I said, eager to give her a victory. I see her face now, as I write. I see the consolation of a single addition to my stock. "What would I have done without this?" I cried convincingly. "Mr. MacPherson would never have forgiven me if I had gone off without it, and the people at the Faustroll Institute might not even have let me enroll if I didn't have it with me. Thanks, Mom."

I meant it, not thanks for Faustroll, but thanks for everything, everything she had ever done for me, including sewing those snappy name tags on my underwear.

The poignance of the moment threatened to overwhelm us. Even my father found it necessary to blow his nose. Before we could make a scene that would embarrass us in the neighborhood, though, a car came to a screeching halt in front of our house. The three of us spun toward the street and saw Rocco's T-Bucket sliding to a stop. Patti Fiorenza got out and hurried toward us with a poster in her hand. "These are all over town," she said, waving the poster at me.

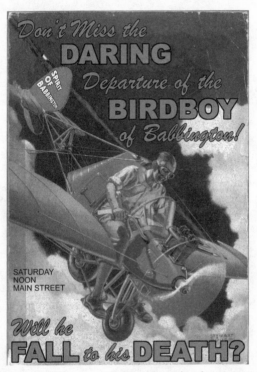

"These are all over town," she said, waving the poster at me.

Chapter 49
Albertine's Childlike State of Wonder and Receptivity

A VASE OF FLOWERS was on Albertine's bedside table, another on the rolling table that held her meals and books, and more flowers at the foot of her bed, on a small table that held equipment for the nurses.

"This is nice," I said, indicating the flowers. "Friends and family checking in?"

"Yes," she said, "but most of the flowers are from the flyguys."

"Oh," I said. "Of course."

"Peter—"

"You're going to tell me that you've decided to run off with the flyguys?"

"What?"

"You're not, are you?"

"Don't be ridiculous."

"They've got that swagger."

"Don't be silly," she said with a giggle that I'd have to call involuntary, possibly irrepressible. "I was going to ask you if you have any plans for planes that seem as if they might really fly."

"Like the Pinch-a-Penny?" I asked, to cover a secret sigh of relief.

"Not at all like the Pinch-a-Penny. Something that appears to be aerodynamically sound and doesn't seem likely to fall apart at the wrong time."

"At the wrong time?"

"In the middle of an Immelmann turn, for example."

"There are some."

"Are there any that we could actually build—you and I?"

I wasn't accustomed to being asked to consider what would be required to realize a dream that I thought of as "only a dream." I needed a moment to think, so I said, "Hmmm," put my hand on my chin, and walked to the window. After a long moment's consideration, I said, "Yes."

"But?"

"But those tend to be expensive. The ones that you'd be interested in, willing to fly in, aren't the ones that the builder builds from scratch."

"The ones built from scratch are the ones with the graceful lines of coffins."

"Right. The sleek ones are built from kits, with the smooth parts made in a factory somewhere."

"So there wouldn't be as much work for the fun couple?"

"From what I've seen, I think there's plenty of work involved in assembling even the most complete kit. Besides, the fun couple would have to do some work to scare up the money to buy the kit."

"Suppose we ignore that for the time being."

"You sound like me, my darling."

"I do, don't I? But still, I wish you would bring me some pictures. I'd like to explore the idea a bit. I think I've got the urge to build a plane."

"Where on earth could that have come from?"

"I don't know," she said, and she seemed bewildered, as if she actually didn't know, as if the swaggering flyguys had nothing to do with it. "Maybe I'm only dreaming—daydreaming or nightdreaming—it's hard to tell here in the hospital, with the drugs and the way people come and go. I read, and then I doze, and I dream, and then I seem to wake, but later, when I actually do wake, I wonder whether I really was awake earlier, or only dreaming that I was awake, but more and more I find myself dreaming of flying—no, that's not right—I find myself dreaming of the two of us building a plane."

"We still don't have a garage," I reminded her.

"I like the idea of our working together," she said, ignoring the impediment to our doing so that the lack of a garage represented.

"So do I," I said.

An awkward silence fell. An unasked question was in the room, stalking us like a mosquito.

"Did you—the walker—the test?" I asked.

"No," she said, frowning. "I walked a few steps, and then the pain and the strain were just too much for me. I got woozy. I had to stop."

"Oh."

ON THE WAY HOME, I turned toward the river again, walked east to the railing at the edge of Carl Schurz Park, and walked along it, northward, homeward, but listlessly. I wasn't in any hurry to return to the empty apartment. After a while I began to think that I heard footsteps behind me, raising questions of strategy. Would it be best to speed up, walk at a pace brisk enough to get me away from whoever was behind me, or to assume the attitude that Al and I call "tough and crazy" in an attempt to get the stalker to walk off at a pace brisk enough to get him away from me, or simply to stop, turn, and confront this other nighttime walker as if he were as harmless as I?

I stopped. I turned. I found myself confronting a guy known in the neighborhood as Baudelaire because of his uncanny resemblance to Nadar's portrait photograph of 1863. Baudelaire always walked tough and crazy, but he was as harmless as I.

"How's the sweet patootie?" he asked.

"She's—do you know that she's in the hospital?"

"Sure. It's all over the neighborhood. I sent her flowers."

"You did?"

"You find that hard to believe?"

"No. Not at all. It's just—"

"Hard to believe. Okay, it was a joint gift. I chipped in."

I was tempted to ask him where he had gotten money to chip in. It was hard to believe that he was gainfully employed. On the other hand, perhaps he was. Perhaps he was paid by the city to walk the neighborhood at all hours like a brooding zombie. There might have been a New York City Department of Brooding Zombies, lightly funded but with a few dollars to give out. I didn't ask. Perhaps I didn't want to know.

"Those flowers frightened me," I said.

He gave me a wary look and drew an inch or so away from me. "The flowers frightened you?" he asked.

"Yeah," I said. "Not yours, but bunches of flowers that came from the flyguys. When I saw them there, for a horrible moment I feared that Al was going to tell me she'd decided to run off with the flyguys. One of them, anyway."

"I'm not acquainted with the flyguys."

"They're paramedics—emergency medical technicians—EMTs—but they fly helicopters instead of driving ambulances."

"I see."

"They swagger."

"Oh," he said sympathetically.

"Worse than that, they've *got* swagger. Even when they're not actually swaggering, you can see that at any moment they could swagger if they chose to, without breaking a sweat." I paused. I leaned on the railing. I exhaled. "I think Albertine is infatuated with them."

"It may be nothing more than a symptom of the phenomenon of convalescence," he suggested.

"Really?" I asked hopefully.

"Convalescence," he said, apparently musing on the subject as he spoke, "is like a return toward childhood. The convalescent, like the child, is possessed in the highest degree of the faculty of keenly interesting himself in things, be they apparently of the most trivial."

"Mm," I agreed.

"Let us go back, if we can, by a retrospective effort of the imagination—"

"A thought experiment?"

"If you like. Let us go back toward our most youthful, our earliest, impressions, and we will recognize that they have a strange kinship with those

. . . his uncanny resemblance to Nadar's portrait photograph of 1863.

brightly colored impressions that we receive in the aftermath of a physical illness."

Side by side, looking out at the dark water, we made that retrospective effort of the imagination.

"Yeah," I said after a while. "I see what you mean," though in truth I hadn't experienced or rediscovered the kinship with impressions after an illness of which he had spoken because, standing there, under pressure to bring to mind an illness and its aftermath and the impressions that I had had in its aftermath, I couldn't remember any impressions after any illness. I couldn't even remember any illnesses. Memory, as Proust said in so many words, resists the demands we make on it, does not want to be brought onstage before it has its makeup on right.

"Provided, of course," he continued, "that the illness has left our spiritual capacities pure and unharmed."

"Of course."

"The child sees everything in a state of newness; he is always drunk."

"In this case, she."

"She. Yes. Nothing more resembles what we call inspiration than the delight with which a child absorbs form and color."

"Or appreciates swagger."

"Or anything else."

"So her interest in the flyguys, in flying, in building a plane, might only be symptoms or characteristics of the childlike state of wonder and receptivity that convalescence has put her in."

"Yes, I think that may be. Or she may be one of those who have the ability to recover childhood at will, to regain that state of newness."

"I've been told that I—"

"That ability is nothing more nor less than genius, I think."

We watched the water in silence for a while longer.

"What have you been told that you—?" he asked.

"Oh, nothing," I said. I held out my hand. "Thanks for sending the flowers."

"Chipping in," he corrected.

"Right. Thanks."

"She's a sweetie," he said, and with a wave that I'm tempted to call jaunty, he went on his way. I went on mine.

Chapter 50
A Banner Day

SATURDAY CAME, the day of my departure, and I was ready. I felt ready, and I knew that I really was ready. I felt that, overnight, I had changed: I had become an adventurer, a daring adventurer, an outstanding example of the type, in the teen division. As I ate breakfast, I seemed to detect in the manner of my eating the manner common to all great adventurers on the mornings when they set out on, well, their great adventures. I had cocoa and buttered toast, and I told myself to remember the fact, because what I ate on the morning of my setting out was somehow significant, that *everything* I did now was somehow significant, a part of the exploits of the Birdboy of Babbington. Having eaten, and having filled myself with self-importance, I stepped out the kitchen door and discovered, assembled in our driveway, everyone who had worked on the aerocycle. Under their admiring gaze, I descended the steps, crossed the bit of packed earth beside the back stoop—a patch of ground that never would sustain a covering of grass—crunched across the driveway, and mounted the aerocycle. For those few steps, I may have swaggered.

For a while I just sat there on my machine, in the driveway in front of the garage, while my friends applauded me, or their handiwork, or both, and I applauded them. Then I said a few words of thanks.

"I don't know how to thank you," I began, and though so many other people in similar situations had said that, it was, I think, no less true for its being the expected thing. "You took my dream and made it a reality," I went on. "Without your work, I wouldn't have been able to do more than *imagine* a trip to the Land of Enchantment—but, thanks to you, I'm really going."

I intended to say more. I wanted to spend some time discoursing on the inestimable value of friendship, on the type of debt that can never be repaid, on the acknowledgment that adventurers owe to all the little people whose efforts make their ventures possible, that sort of thing. But I was interrupted by the arrival of Porky White, my sponsor.

Porky's delivery van rumbled up and shuddered to a sagging stop at the edge of the road, and Porky clambered out, shouting, "Not yet! Don't start yet!"

He ran around to the back of the van, opened the doors, and began tugging at something inside.

"You can't go without the banner," he called. He grabbed Matthew Barber, handed one end of the banner to him, and said, "Here. Unroll this." Matthew began backing up, unrolling the banner. Porky had tied wooden uprights into the banner at intervals to keep the upper line and the lower line separated and the letters upstanding. When Matthew was about thirty-five feet away, the message was revealed:

KAP'N KLAM IS COMING! THE HOME OF HAPPY DINNERS!

"I made it myself," said Porky with pride.

"It's, um, it—" I mumbled.

"What?"

"It's supposed to say 'THE HOME OF HAPPY DINERS.'"

"Yeah. It does."

"Well, no. It says, 'HAPPY DINNERS.'"

"Huh?"

"Actually, it says, 'YPPAH SRENNID,'" said Marvin Jones, from the other side of the banner.

"You've got one too many *n*'s," I pointed out.

"Oh," said Porky. "Shit."

"Porky!" said my mother.

"Sorry. I just—it's just that it's important to me. I've got a lot riding on this, you know? My hopes and dreams are going up there with Peter, and—"

"Maybe it doesn't matter," I suggested. "Why not 'happy dinners'? Maybe it's happy dinners that make happy diners."

"Dinners cannot be happy," said Matthew. "Diners can be happy. Dinners cannot. Dinners are meals. Meals are inanimate. They have no emotions. They cannot be happy."

"They can make people happy."

"Yes, they can, but they cannot themselves be made happy."

"An occasion can be happy," I asserted. "This is a happy occasion."

"It was," grumbled my father.

"Yes, an occasion can be happy," Matthew conceded.

"Isn't a meal an occasion?" I asked.

"Not quite. A meal is something that occupies an occasion. It is not itself an occasion. Consider the analogy of a headache—"

"That's what I'm getting," said Porky.

"A headache occupies a period of time," asserted Matthew, "but is not itself a period of time. Similarly, a meal occupies a period of time but is not itself a period of time. A meal is like a headache—"

"I'm getting one, too," said my father.

"—in that it occupies a period of time and during that time may arouse emotion in beings capable of feeling emotion. The emotion, however, is in the sentient beings, not in the activity. Thus, to speak of a 'happy meal' is an absurdity."

"Fixed!" announced my mother with a flourish, like a wizard. "I just snipped out one *n* and sewed the pieces together."

"Ella!" cried Porky, sweeping her up in a bear hug. "Thank you, thank you, thank you. You are amazing." Swinging her in his arms, he called out to everyone there, "Isn't she amazing?"

We cheered her until she hid her face in her hands, then Porky set her down beside my scowling father and said to me, "We've got to attach this to the back of the plane."

"Aerocycle," I corrected him.

"Right," he said. "I brought wire."

Porky and I wired the banner to the rear of the aerocycle while everyone else watched. When at last the operation was done, I was truly ready to go.

I remounted the aerocycle, pulled my goggles over my eyes, stood up, and came down hard on the kick-starter. The engine roared into life. The propeller began to turn. Dust and pebbles whirled in the air and drove the circle of my friends and supporters outward. I rolled forward, down the driveway, toward the street.

The aerocycle was, I found to my immense relief, quite easy to maneuver on the ground. I had had some concern about this, inspired by my reading of Pope and Otis. They warned the readers of *Elements of Aeronautics* that most light planes of that time were difficult to control on the ground because they were steered by the same control surfaces that steered them in the air—the rudder and ailerons. Those controls functioned well in the air, at flying speeds, but barely at all on the ground, at taxiing speeds. The aerocycle, however, retained its motorcycle handlebars, and they turned its front wheel in addition to its rudder and ailerons, making it easily maneuverable. I knew how to ride a bicycle, so I found that the aerocycle felt familiar, and I could steer it well enough to avoid running into my friends.

In the street, I turned toward the south, toward Main Street, where I planned to make my takeoff.

Chapter 51
Pleasure and Pain, in Sympathy

WACKO WOKE ME, chirping at me in that eager way he has. Wacko is the alarm clock that I keep on my bedside table. That is, "Wacko" is what Albertine and I call the alarm clock that I keep on my bedside table. The manufacturer of the clock called it Whack-It, not Wacko, but that was because the manufacturer did not, I think, have the degree of familiarity with the device that Al and I have, a degree of familiarity that we've developed over the fifteen years that we've owned him (yes, him). Wacko is a personality in our lives. He wakes us every weekday morning with that chirping sound, full of pep and vigor, keen to get at the day and conquer it, and then I reach out and whack him to shut him up, as the manufacturer's instructions encouraged me to do. The whack-to-silence feature was what led the manufacturer to name him Whack-It, but after he became a member of our household, Wacko earned his nickname by insisting that time passes more quickly for him than for other clocks. He is a tiny digital clock, controlled by a chip, and he should be stable and accurate, yet he gains about a minute a day, and his attitude toward his inaccuracy is of the dismissive shrug and "so what?" variety.

I whacked him. I fumbled for the slide switch and turned his alarm off. I opened my eyes. They stung. I closed them again. I stretched and let my head fall back on the pillow.

Time passed, no more than a minute or two, I thought. Little by little, I urged my eyes open. The bedroom was bright with sunlight. I glanced at Wacko. According to him, an hour and a half had passed. Suddenly, in the moment of my looking at Wacko's digital display, I remembered a dream, a dream about Albertine. We had been together, in bed, doing delightful things to each other. It was a tremendously erotic moment of recollection, and the dream was as arousing in the memory as it must have been in the dreaming, but the most intriguing aspect of the dream was that it was actually a dream about dreaming. In it, I had been dreaming; I had been a dreamer dreaming of being in bed with Albertine, and that distance between me the dreamer and me the lover made it seem as if my being in bed with her was somehow illicit. It was all so deliciously erotic that I, the I who was the dreamer dreaming of making love to Albertine, wanted to wake up in the middle of it, to get out of the dream.

"Why?" I can almost hear you asking. "Why would you want to wake up in the middle of a gloriously erotic dream and end it?"

So that I could tell Albertine about it, of course.

I knew that she would enjoy an account of it—that is, within the dream, the dreaming I (Peter the Second) knew that she would—and so within the dream Peter the Second forced himself to wake up, ending his dream (in which he was enjoying Albertine as Peter the Third), and, still in my (Peter the First's) dream, he (Peter the Second), now awake, reached out for Albertine, and there she was beside him, and he nuzzled her and said, in a whisper, "I had a dream, a dream about you."

She stretched herself, drew herself alongside him, caressed him and extended, lasciviously, that most generous of invitations: "Tell me all about it."

Then Wacko began his cheery chirping and woke me, Peter the First, from my dream.

But wait. That waking must have been within the dream as well, because Wacko was there on the bedside table, with his alarm turned off. There must have been Peters One through Four . . .

This was definitely something that I had to tell Al.

I swung myself to the edge of the bed, swung my legs to the floor, and put my weight on my legs, standing, as we human beings have been doing for some time now, and a pain shot through my right leg, a pain so severe and so totally unexpected that the leg collapsed under me, and I had to throw myself back on the bed to keep from falling to the floor.

I was overjoyed.

"Albertine," I called out to the empty apartment, "I feel your pain!"

Chapter 52
Albertine Takes Off

I HAD TOLD MYSELF, often, that it would not be a good idea to enter
the hospital through the emergency entrance, where the flyguys were
likely to be, that the wise course would be to use the main entrance and to
avoid the flyguys if I saw them, but desire—or need—opposed that wisdom. I wanted—or needed—to measure myself against them. I suppose
that I also hoped that by observing them I might pick up some of their
swagger or—even better—that I might learn the art of swagger itself and
so develop a swagger that I could call my own, a swagger that Albertine
would find even more attractive than flyguy swagger.

It seems to me, by the way, that *swagger* is not entirely a complimen-
tary term. It's just a letter away from *stagger,* for one thing, and I seem to
hear an echo of *braggart.* The term *swagger* may (one of my dictionaries
says "may possibly," which I take to mean "probably doesn't") derive ultimately from the Norwegian *svaga,* which gives us *swag,* meaning a
swaying or lurching movement, which suggests to me the walk of a sailor
who hasn't regained his land legs after a voyage, or who after a long life
at sea affects in landlubberly retirement the rolling gait he used to use on
the moving surface of a deck, or who is drunk.

The emergency entrance, at the corner of "our" street, the street
where "our" apartment building was located, was the quickest way into
the hospital, and so, instead of doing the wise thing and continuing
around the corner to the main entrance, I limped through the emergency
entrance, favoring the leg with the sympathetic pain. The flyguys were
there, right there, standing in a group, drinking coffee, managing some-

how to exhibit swagger while standing still. I put my head down and made my way to the elevator. I pressed the button and waited. When the doors opened, I staggered in, and suddenly the flyguys crowded in with me. I reached for the button for the sixth floor, Albertine's floor, but one of them beat me to it.

"How's it goin'?" he asked me after pressing the button.

"Huh?" I replied, surprised by the question, the attention, the notice.

"How you doin'?"

"Me?"

"Yeah. I've seen you here before, right?"

"I—"

"Our floor," said a flyguy in the back.

We got off, and we walked toward Albertine's room as if we were a group.

"My darling," I said as I stepped through the door, "I had the most amazing—"

"I passed!" she squealed.

"Way to go, Giggles!" boomed a hearty flyguy from over my shoulder.

"The Walker Test?" I asked, and then I added, "Did he call you Giggles?"

"This morning," she said. "I tried to call you, but there was no answer. I told them that Giggle Bars are my favorite candy."

"Hoo-rah, Giggles, hoo-rah, Giggles," boomed the flyguy chorus.

"Oh," I said. "I must have been on my way here when you called. Or maybe I was asleep. Wacko—"

"Ready to go home?" asked a hearty flyguy, pushing past me with a wheelchair.

"Am I!" cried Giggles. She began sliding from the bed into the wheelchair that the flyguy was holding steady for her.

"We'll take it from here, sport," said another of them, clapping a firm hand on my shoulder.

"I'm her husband," I said, as if it were a conjurer's formula for effecting disappearance.

"The hapless dreamer!" said the wheelchair jockey, standing and frankly staring in my direction.

"I told them that's what you call yourself sometimes," said Albertine. She blushed. Reader, she blushed.

"*Entre nous,* I thought," I said. I pouted. Reader, I pouted.

"I was under the influence of drugs."

"And swagger," I said, mostly to myself.

"Didn't they used to call you the Birdboy of Babbington, back in the old days?" asked the wheelchair guy.

"Well, yes—"

"Holy shit. You were my inspiration."

"I was?"

"My parents used to tell me about you when I was a kid, growing up on Long Island. You were a legend."

"Well—"

"I was inspired by your example."

"Were you?"

"Hell, yes! Because of you, I built a small jet, using surplus parts."

"A jet?"

"Just a small one."

"We're going to give Giggles a lift," said the flyguy with the grip on my shoulder.

"We live just down the street," I said. "I can push her."

"Sure you can—but why not enhance the experience?"

"Yeah," said another. "Why should she be going home in a wheelchair when she can be going home in an XP-99 chopper?"

"That'll make it a thrill, not a walk."

"It will be fun for me, Peter," said Albertine, as if she were asking permission to stay out after curfew.

"But where are you going to land?" I asked. "The courtyard inside our building is too small, I think, and there are lots of trees—"

"We're going to land on the roof."

"Of our building?"

"Of the hospital."

"This hospital?"

"Sure!" said one, as if only an earthbound idiot could have asked such a question.

"You're going to take off from here, and then land here?"

"We'll take off, take a spin around Manhattan, and then we'll come back and land."

"And then what?"

"What do you mean?"

"How does she get home from here?"

"You can push her in the wheelchair."

"That was my original idea."

"But the experience will have been enhanced."

We took the elevator to the roof. Along the way, I had to suffer the deference that everyone paid to the flyguys. Even the surgeons, who had a type of swagger of their own, seemed to shrink a bit in their presence.

They loaded her into the helicopter. She waved, smiling like a little girl. They took off, banked, and headed south, over the river.

Chapter 53
I Take Off

MY DEPARTURE from Babbington was everything that I could have wished it to be. As I rolled southward from my house in Babbington Heights, I saw, here and there, people standing at the curbside, waving. Now and then a parent would bend to a child and point at me and say something that I couldn't hear. Of course, I allowed myself to think that the words I wasn't hearing were words of praise for me, for my pluck and enterprise and ingenuity. I may have heard, uttered in a hushed tone of awed admiration, the epithet "Birdboy of Babbington," but I am sure that I never heard anything that sounded remotely like "birdbrain."

By the time I reached the intersection with Main Street, where I intended to turn right and head west, the people gathered along the roadside had become quite a crowd. Across the intersection there was, at that time, an empty lot, just a bit of long grass. In that lot, a small platform had been erected, and on the platform stood the mayor of Babbington himself.

As I approached the intersection, I suddenly found myself surrounded by motorcycle cops. I thought I was being arrested.

"Do you have a license to fly that thing?" asked one of the cops.

"Heck," I said with all the bravado I could manage, "I don't even have a license to *drive* this thing!"

They roared at that. At least I think they did. They seemed to be laughing, and their motorcycles roared.

One of the cops pointed in the direction of the platform, and I understood then that I was expected to stop there and allow the mayor to give me a send-off. That was fine with me, because standing beside the mayor was Miss

Clam Fest, a young beauty just a couple of years out of high school but already more woman than girl, wearing a white bathing suit with her Miss Clam Fest banner draped across her alluring figure. I headed straight for her.

The mayor intercepted me, putting a firm hand on my shoulder, turning me toward the crowd, and announcing, "Citizens of Babbington, here is your Birdboy, Peter—ah—Lee-roy."

The applause was friendly, but light.

"Citizens of Babbington, fellow Babbingtonians, denizens of our cozy bayside community, friends and neighbors," said the mayor, to the best of my recollection, "we are about to witness something truly extraordinary. We are about to witness the fulfillment of a dream. This boy, our own Peter Lee-roy, had a dream, the dream of flight. Who among us has not had that dream? Peter, however, has done something that most of us will never do. He has had the—dare I say it?—gumption to put wings on his dream. To put wings on it, wheels under it, and an engine on the front of it. In other words, he has taken that dream and made it a blueprint for reality. Now, many people criticize our public schools."

A critical murmur spread through the crowd.

"Hardly a day goes by without some crank letter arriving in my office filled with groundless complaints about the collapse of standards in the schools. Well, let me tell you something: this plucky lad is a product of those schools. And I think we can be proud of him."

A smattering of applause.

"His teachers tell me—and he may be surprised to find that I've been doing a little checking up on him—that he's an imaginative boy, inclined to dream, often distracted, and prone to digression, but they are convinced that he's got a head on his shoulders. Perhaps that is why they recommended him wholeheartedly for a summer session at the prestigious Faustroll Institute in distant New Mexico, Land of Enchantment."

The mayor paused, turned slightly toward me, and applauded me in a formal, rather than enthusiastic, way. The crowd took the cue and applauded as well, and Miss Clam Fest blew me a kiss. I wondered if she would fit on the seat behind me and whether she had ever been to New Mexico.

"And so," said the mayor, "one of our own leaves today to prepare himself for the great struggle that we as a nation are engaged in, the struggle to make the world safe for democracy. Young Peter and those other bright-eyed young men—and young women—like him—including—ah—"

He consulted a sheet of paper.

"—Matthew Barber—"

He shaded his eyes and looked out at the crowd. Matthew, a couple of rows back, raised his hand, and memory—injecting a recollection from the third grade—made me think for a moment that he was going to ask to go to the bathroom.

"—who will be attending a summer institute for future pharmacists, coincidentally also in New Mexico, although Matthew will be traveling by regularly scheduled commercial airliner—they are the bright hope of a nation facing a foe with incomprehensible animosities and aims, a foe purely and simply evil. Perhaps it should come as no surprise, then, to learn that Peter has received a communication from the federal government in Washington—which his mother kindly brought to my attention—wishing him, and I quote, 'the best of luck in your . . . endeavors.'"

He paused. He gripped my shoulder more tightly. He set his jaw.

"Our hopes ride with him," he said.

The hopes of the nation should have felt like too great a burden for a kid to bear, too heavy a weight of responsibility for the *Spirit of Babbington* to get off the ground, but I relished the burden, since it made Miss Clam Fest smile and sigh and flutter her lashes.

In something of a daze, I made my way through a phalanx of cops to the aerocycle. The applause now was really something, loud and genuine. I had become the teenage hero of my cozy bayside community. I felt admired, and I felt that I deserved admiration. I felt capable and strong and daring.

I mounted the aerocycle, came down hard on the kick-starter, and rode off into the sunset, or into the direction of the place where sunset would occur later that evening, with the Kap'n Klam banner clattering behind me.

TO BE CONTINUED

*Will Peter fly the aerocycle all the way to the
Land of Enchantment?*

Will the flyguys return Albertine
as promised?

*Will Peter matriculate at the prestigious
Faustroll Institute?*

Or will he
FALL
to his
DEATH?

*Don't miss
the thrilling continuation
of
Peter and Albertine's exploits
in*

Flying
Part 2: On the Wing